The hit was going down in Chinatown

Bolan and Trevans raced toward the man in the overcoat. He saw them and turned to walk away, his coat flashing open to reveal the barrel of a shotgun.

'Stop right there!'' Bolan shouted, jerking Big Thunder from its combat harness.

The man started to raise his hands as Bolan approached cautiously. Suddenly Trevans pushed the Executioner hard, knocking him to the ground. 'Watch out!''

Bolan fell, rolling, and saw a man in a second-story window with an automatic. The assassin's bullets chewed up the sidewalk and chopped into Trevans chest-high. Bolan let loose a burst that spun the man around and pitched him through the opening.

Then he moved to where Carl Trevans lay and knelt beside the broken body. He was dead, killed by bullets meant for Bolan.

'He was a good man,'' a voice said above him.

Bolan looked up. "What would you know about it?''

MACK BOLAN

The Executioner

DON PENDLETON's EXECUTIONER
MACK BOLAN
American Nightmare

A GOLD EAGLE BOOK FROM
W☾RLDWIDE

TORONTO • NEW YORK • LONDON • PARIS
AMSTERDAM • STOCKHOLM • HAMBURG
ATHENS • MILAN • TOKYO • SYDNEY

First edition November 1987

ISBN 0-373-61107-2

Special thanks and acknowledgment to
Mike McQuay for his contribution to this work.

Printed in Canada

No passion so effective robs the mind of all its powers of acting and reasoning as fear.

—Edmund Burke

Life only demands from you the strength you possess. Only one feat is possible—not to have run away.

—Mack Bolan

THE
MACK BOLAN
LEGEND

Nothing less than a war could have fashioned the destiny of the man called Mack Bolan. Bolan earned the Executioner title in the jungle hell of Vietnam.

But this soldier also wore another name—Sergeant Mercy. He was so tagged because of the compassion he showed to wounded comrades-in-arms and Vietnamese civilians.

Mack Bolan's second tour of duty ended prematurely when he was given emergency leave to return home and bury his family, victims of the Mob. Then he declared a one-man war against the Mafia.

He confronted the Families head-on from coast to coast, and soon a hope of victory began to appear. But Bolan had broken society's every rule. That same society started gunning for this elusive warrior—to no avail.

So Bolan was offered amnesty to work within the system against terrorism. This time, as an employee of Uncle Sam, Bolan became Colonel John Phoenix. With a command center at Stony Man Farm in Virginia, he and his new allies—Able Team and Phoenix Force—waged relentless war on a new adversary: the KGB.

But when his one true love, April Rose, died at the hands of the Soviet terror machine, Bolan severed all ties with Establishment authority.

Now, after a lengthy lone-wolf struggle and much soul-searching, the Executioner has agreed to enter an "arm's-length" alliance with his government once more, reserving the right to pursue personal missions in his Everlasting War.

PROLOGUE

Northern Africa

His mother, perhaps, had contracted measles while pregnant with him, or perhaps she had smoked too much or the baby had been choked by his umbilical cord, cutting off oxygen to the brain. Perhaps he was simply a product of his conditioning, the same sort of conditioning that he, himself, used to great advantage. Whatever had gutted the humanity from the man had done a complete job. He was called a man purely for biological reasons, for lack of another word to call him. He was called a man because human language had never invented a word for what he really was.

"Do you see?" the colonel asked him as they surveyed the cordoned-off wreckage of what had once been the presidential palace. "Do you see what they do to me...to my family?"

The man in the impeccable white suit looked, and he saw. The F-111s had done a good job of precision bombing in the dead of night, picking up their targets purely on computer enhancement, getting in through a barrage of antiaircraft fire and getting away almost clean despite a sky heavy with flak. It had been a successful mission, a bit showy, perhaps, but effective nonetheless. For his money, however, the best bet would have simply been to hire the right finger to drop the hammer on the man who was sitting beside him at the moment. Governments always complicated the simple.

"A terrible thing," he said.

The colonel fixed him with a searching look, and he thought he detected a hint of madness in the Arab's brown eyes.

"The devils have killed my children," the colonel said, his blue *ghutra* a marked contrast to the khaki of his uniform and his sun-bronzed skin. "They came in the night like the cowards they are, taking the blood of innocents, trying to undermine the just power with which I rule my people, my children."

The man stood, binoculars in hand, and surveyed the devastation from above the windshield. The palace had been demolished, and nothing remained other than several pillars surrounded by tons of rubble—everything within a square kilometer had been wasted. It had been a good operation, but not perfect. The only thing that really amazed him was that it was still there. "Aren't you going to clean it up?" he asked the colonel.

"No," the Arab responded. "This is our shrine, the people's reminder of the devils who sit waiting to pounce should we cease our vigilance. Doesn't the sight of this make you burn with the fires of anger?"

The man sat down and handed the binoculars back to the colonel. "My job calls for a cool head, not hot blood. That's why you hired me."

The colonel stared at him, frowning deeply. Then slowly, very slowly, a smile spread across his face. "You may be a man I think I can understand," he said, and put the jeep into gear while giving a "move out" sign to the driver of the personnel carrier parked next to them. He turned the jeep around and headed through the profusion of white-plastered homes that made up this mostly residential area of the port city of Tripoli.

The late-afternoon heat was oppressive. Dust rose in thick, choking clouds, and the man rode with a handkerchief pressed tightly to nose and mouth. He went by the name of Blocker when doing business. It wasn't his real name, but one that served his purpose.

"You are a businessman!" the colonel said loudly so that he could be heard above the noises of his entourage. "You simply have a job to do!"

Blocker merely nodded, all the while aware of the fact that the colonel had absolutely no idea of what he was like. On the other hand, the visit to the ruins told him more than he'd ever need to know about the colonel, and convinced him more than ever that the bulk of their agreement would have to be paid up front.

"Do you think this matter will give you much trouble?" the colonel asked him.

The man shrugged. "On the whole I don't think so. America has never known real terrorism and foolishly thinks itself immune. On the other hand, its population is violent and well-armed. Any trouble I have may come from unseen complications in dealing with its citizens. It's nothing I can't handle."

"For the right money."

"If you thought your own people could do it, you wouldn't have come to me."

The colonel visibly tensed, angered by the implied insult, and several seconds passed before he relaxed. "Does the job frighten you?"

"No," Blocker answered quickly.

"Will you work alone?"

"Our agreement was, no questions about my methods."

"Fair enough."

They drove the harbor road to their next destination, the waters of the Mediterranean sparkling blue-green under a blazing sun. Within fifteen minutes they had pulled up to the huge gates of regimental army headquarters. The gates were swung open, and the colonel drove into the large, walled courtyard.

He leaped from the driver's seat and removed his cap, wiping his forehead on the sleeve of his uniform. The man in the white suit didn't sweat much. He was lean, all muscle and sinew. He had nothing to sweat away.

"Before we seal our bargain, Mr. Blocker," the colonel said, "I have something I want to show you."

The man smiled, turning his eyes heavenward. "Something inside, I hope."

The colonel laughed, an unnatural, forced laugh, the kind of laugh that people who have no sense of humor trot out on occasion. "It will be outside, my friend, but it won't take long."

The colonel signaled toward the headquarters building, where an apparently prearranged activity was about to take place. "Come," he said. "We'll escape the sun just a little."

He led Blocker toward one of the fifty-foot courtyard walls. They moved into its shadow just as a corporal ran up to them with two small cups of bitter cardamom coffee.

As they sipped the black brew, they watched three men, obviously prisoners, being led in chains across the courtyard by a small squad carrying AK-47s on their shoulders.

The men, their clothes torn and dirty, were brought close to where the colonel and Blocker stood, then were made to stand against the wall. They were Caucasian, possibly American.

"My little surprise," the colonel stated proudly. "Three slightly used tools of Satan, purchased from my brothers in Beirut."

"American hostages," Blocker surmised. "What did they cost you?"

"A million each," came the response. "A worthwhile price. Money means nothing to me."

"And why do you show them to me?"

The colonel's face became hard as he took the cup from Blocker's hand and dropped it on the ground. "You are the one with all the answers," he said, "the man with all the poise. Maybe you would like to tell me."

The man smiled. "I assure you that I am here completely at your disposal and good graces. I am simply a cog in your wheel, and an unworthy cog at that."

The colonel smiled in return. "These men are Americans...your countrymen. What are your feelings toward them?"

"I have no feelings toward them," the man said shortly.

"Perhaps if you studied them more closely." The colonel guided Blocker by the arm until he stood before the three men. They had been beaten, their faces and arms covered with bruises and open, festering sores. They smelled of rot and death. They looked at the man with pleading eyes, the only spark of life left in them.

"A teacher," the colonel said, pointing to the first man, "teaching capitalist evil to impressionable children." He pointed to the second. "A banker, stealing money from the poor of Lebanon. And a minister, preaching the American Satan to good Muslims. A holy man, Mr. Blocker. You have no feelings for your holy men?"

Blocker simply stared at him, his gaze unwavering, neither passive nor aggressive. He perceived a test in the making.

The Arab drew his nickle-plated .357 Magnum from its holster. Ten feet distant, the line of infantry primed their weapons, pointing them skyward. The colonel handed the gun to his companion. "You will prove your loyalty to me by shooting these men," he said.

"No," the man said flatly.

"You refuse?" the colonel asked angrily.

"This is business. I don't do business for free."

The colonel barked orders to the soldiers, who trained their guns on the man in the white suit. "You will shoot these men now, Mr. Blocker, or join them on the other side.''

The man never wavered. "I am a professional," he said. "You brought me here because of my professional reputation, which is sterling. Now you ask me to throw my professionalism out the window and show you my so-called loyalty at the point of a gun. What would such a display prove, except that I'm not as good as you heard? I will be more than happy to dispatch your prisoners for you, should you meet my price. If not, you will have to shoot me now and end what has turned into a ridiculous controversy. The choice is yours, for my business sense has determined my choice."

The colonel shook his head, then motioned for his men to lower their weapons. "What is your price?" he asked.

"Twenty-five thousand dollars," the man said, "on top of our other deal. A waste of money, I'd say, when you could as easily do it yourself."

The colonel thought for a moment; one of the prisoners groaned loudly and fell to the ground. "Perhaps just one," he said. "One would be a good test...and cheaper."

"A deal, then?" the man asked.

"A deal. Should my accountant...?"

"I trust your word," the man said. "Which one?"

"The minister of Satan."

Blocker nodded, but handed back the colonel's gun. Instead, he reached toward the ten-inch blade that was strapped to the chieftain's boot. He unsnapped it, enjoying the feel of the bone handle.

He moved easily to the minister and cut off his pants, leaving him naked from the waist down. As the man screamed, he castrated him, an act done to show his employer that he was sending the minister to Allah unclean. Then he gutted the man from sternum to pelvis, spilling his insides onto the dusty ground, the man's final prayers twisting through his lips as a scream.

He then wiped the blade on the dead man's clothes and handed it back.

"Excellent."

"I always give good dollar value," Blocker replied.

The colonel nodded. "We will do business now."

The other two men were shot by the soldiers as Blocker and his employer crossed the courtyard to the wide steps that led to the barracks. Within minutes they were sitting in the colonel's air-conditioned office with his accountant.

The office was large and messy, with loose papers and file boxes scattered everywhere, the signs of a man constantly on the move. Blocker had to move a huge stack of printout paper from a chair in order to sit down.

The accountant was grossly overweight. He wore a dark, Western-style business suit and sunglasses, smoked a thin, black cigar and constantly ran a hand over his slick black hair.

The colonel began shifting through the stacks of paper on his desk, angrily throwing them all over the room when he couldn't find what he wanted.

"We have the ten million for you," Rashi, the accountant, said, and placed a large aluminum suitcase on the desktop. "Half now, half after completing the job."

Rashi opened the suitcase and stared at the banded stacks of American money, all twenties. He idly wondered for a moment if five million could really fit in one suitcase.

"I can do nothing with this," Blocker stated flatly.

"What?" the colonel said, distracted.

"I want the money laundered through my IRA sources in Belfast, then deposited in my account in Geneva," the hit man said. "And I don't want half and half. I want eight million up front and the rest later."

"You don't trust me?" the Arab asked, scowling.

"I'll have a great many...expenses," Blocker countered.

The colonel thought for a moment as he continued to look through the papers. "Aha!" he said at last, triumphantly holding up a sheet of paper. He looked at Rashi. "Please do as Mr. Blocker asks. Eight million..."

"And twenty-five thousand," the man added.

"And twenty-five thousand deposited in the Swiss bank," the colonel said. "The rest upon successful completion of this glorious stage of the jihad against Satan. Does that suit you, Mr. Blocker?"

"Quite well," he responded.

The accountant stood, closing the suitcase. No one spoke until he was out of the room.

"I have the list of names," the colonel said as the door closed behind Rashi. He handed over the sheet of paper.

Blocker nodded, his eyebrows arching sharply as he looked at the last name.

"Problems?" the colonel asked.

"You're paying well for the problems," the man replied, reading the list over several times, committing it to memory. He tore up the paper and dropped the pieces in an ashtray on the desk. "Why these people?"

"I have my reasons," the colonel replied, jaw muscles tightening. "Just make sure that responsibility is clearly given."

Blocker picked up a lighter whose base was a hand grenade and flicked it to life, the flame jumping onto the paper in the ashtray and dancing across it in blue and yellow waves.

"Something I don't quite understand," the hit man said, his eyes fixed on the beauty of the flame. "Once I go in and afix responsibility to you, what's to keep the Americans from bombing you the way they did before?"

"Quite simple, Mr. Blocker," the Arab replied. "I will deny it and plead my innocence most loudly. If they don't bomb me, my friends will all know what has happened. If they do, no country in the world will stand behind them. How do your people like to say it...a no-win situation."

"They're not my people," Blocker said, watching intently as the pieces of paper were consumed by the flame.

Mack Bolan geared down to coax the Mercedes up the steep incline, his icy blue eyes searching the stretch of Virginia back roads for signs of an ambush.

The big man wasn't happy. He wasn't happy with the performance of the heavily armored vehicle on the upgrades; he wasn't happy with the training of the two men who rode shotgun with him in the car; he wasn't happy with the season—the explosion of bright green spring colors on the tree-laden mountains all around that made enemy concealment all too easy. The vehicle and the bodyguards he could try to do something about. The season he'd have to live with.

"How about some music?" asked Trevans, the Secret Serviceman beside him in the front seat. He then shifted his riot gun to the floorboards and switched on the radio, filling the car with rock and roll.

"Turn it off," Bolan ordered, resenting the imposition on his battle senses.

"What do you—"

"Turn it off!" Bolan snapped, reaching out to do it himself. "Stay alert. Listen."

Trevans glared at him, seething despite his unruffled countenance. "Listen, hotshot," he said in low tones, hoping to keep the conversation from the

United States senator in the back seat. "You may have shinnied up their pole at Justice, but you're not my boss and I'll be damned if I let you order me around."

Bolan tightened his hands on the wheel and ignored the man, trying instead to concentrate on the road, on the possible danger that lay in wait. If *he* wanted to kidnap or assassinate a man, the isolated stretch of road they were traveling allowed the perfect opportunity for the setup and execution without outside interference.

Trevans was talking to him, but Bolan had tuned him out as he started a long, slow curve up a mountainside. Above Trevans' nasal whine he heard another whine, this one mechanical. He could see nothing in the rearview mirror, but out of the passenger sideview, he could just make out a flash of chrome playing cat-and-mouse behind them.

"A tail," he said to Renfrow, the man in the back seat who was supposed to be covering their rear. "How long has it been there?"

"Hell, I don't know," Renfrow said, twisting in his seat to look through the bulletproof back window. "It's probably—"

"They're going to take us here," Bolan said, reaching into the combat harness he wore under his light jacket and coming out with Big Thunder, his .44 AutoMag. "Hit the door, Renfrow."

"You mean jump?" the man asked.

"Behind those shrubs!" Bolan commanded, pointing to a stand of bushes just off the tree-lined road. "Now! Hit the ground running!"

"But—"

"Do it!"

Renfrow opened the door and jumped—without running on impact. The laws of motion pitched him forward, and he rolled painfully across the asphalt. But he got off the road and hobbled out of sight, Bolan losing him as he rounded the curve and saw a black Lincoln sprawled across the roadway, blocking them.

"Hit the floorboards!" Bolan shouted to Jake Torrance, the senator from Missouri. Then he locked the brakes with both feet, spinning the steering wheel hard left, the Mercedes going into a controlled skid that left it facing the way it had come.

"Oww!" Trevans yelled as Bolan punched the gas. The man was bent over, trying to retrieve his riot gun from the floorboards, his head smashing into the dashboard as Bolan maneuvered the vehicle.

The Mercedes screeched off, speeding head-on toward the car tailing them as gunfire stuttered from behind. The other car came up blind, its driver veering from instinct as it rounded a curve to find the big Merc bearing down on it. It barreled onto the soft shoulder and hit a tree, radiator pumping steam from under the open hood.

Bolan hit the brakes again, the car wreck blocking him off. He skidded to a stop, hitting the door immediately. "Get him into the woods!" he yelled to Trevans, then jumped from the car, Big Thunder in one hand, smoke canister in the other.

He pulled the seal and tossed the bomb down the roadway, even as he heard the roar of the other car's engine as it bore down on him. Then he turned back to the wreck, watching from the corner of his eye as Trevans ran into the woods with Torrance.

Using the car door for cover, he turned Big Thunder on the five men piling out of the wreck as Renfrow came up from the other side to provide a cross fire.

He laid down a pattern of controlled fire and listened to the screech of brakes and the sound of the other car crashing through the branches and underbrush as it lost the road in the thick, white smoke.

"Enough!" came a bullhorn-enhanced voice from within the trees, the order followed by a smattering of applause.

Bolan straightened, reholstering the AutoMag. Smoke was drifting all over the scene as men in uniforms and plainclothes operatives emerged specterlike from hiding in the trees where they had watched the simulation.

As the road began to fill with men, Bolan walked over to the wreck to make sure no one was hurt. All of the men involved in the demonstration were Secret Service and had been training intensively for the past week in counterterrorism techniques under Bolan's watchful eye. It wasn't the kind of work that the big man enjoyed, but in quieter moments he had to admit that, at least for now, it had its value.

The United States was a country for the most part untouched by the fanatical terrorism that had torn Europe and the Middle East apart. Even in its highest echelons of law enforcement and intelligence, the concept of America under terrorist siege was a far-flung and unlikely nightmare. Yet America was a country with wide and open coastlines, its oil production facilities in Texas and Louisiana a soft, vulnerable underbelly upon which the economy depended. It was only a matter of time before maniacs bent on world anarchy through violence and intimidation reached American shores in force.

The Executioner knew the danger was real. He had spent years fighting terrorism in his own way, on his own terms. And though he had spent many of those years as an outlaw himself, his record was solid, his commitments clear. Now, once again, he was working with the blessing of the country he loved, his homeland, working in whatever capacity he was needed in these troubled times. At the moment, that capacity was in the mundane work of training—in this case, the training of Secret Service bodyguards whose job it would be to protect the lives of the men running for the unenviable job of President of the United States in the coming elections.

He moved to the car, a blue Cadillac limo whose front end was wrapped around a tall pine. The last man was getting out of the back seat, a trickle of blood running from his forehead and sliding off his nose to his left cheek.

"You okay, Barnes?" Bolan asked, helping the man onto the road.

"I'm a lot better than if you'd had real bullets in that damned cannon of yours," Steve Barnes replied, grinning.

"You weren't strapped in," Bolan said, checking the man's head to assure himself the wound was superficial.

"Next time," Barnes vowed, taking a handkerchief out of the breast pocket of his dark suit and wiping his wound.

The driver of the limo walked around to where the big man stood, his eyes wide. "You scared the hell out of me," he said, "coming out of nowhere like that. Is there anything else I could have done?"

Bolan shrugged. "You could have tried a one-eighty degree skid and presented him your backside," he answered. "But it might not have helped, or you might not have had the time. It's a judgment call."

"What would you have done?"

Bolan fixed the man with hard eyes. "The same thing I did to you. Gut it out and hope the other guy cracked first."

"That's either very brave or very stupid," came a voice behind Bolan. The big man turned to find himself under the scrutiny of a tall slender man with sandy hair and a friendly face. It was the "real" Senator Jake Torrance.

"It's neither," Bolan replied, reaching out to shake the man's proffered hand. "It's simply an extension of my philosophy regarding terrorism in general—never give an inch. From what I've heard of you, Senator, your philosophy isn't too much different."

"I think that international terrorism is the greatest threat this country will face for the rest of the century," Torrance said, his eyes locking with Bolan's. "I believe that the whole machinery of government needs to be thrown against these people to counteract their fear tactics. By the way, you put on quite a demonstration."

"It was sloppy," Bolan replied, "but thanks just the same."

Renfrow came hobbling by, his pants torn and bloody at the knees. Bolan excused himself from the senator and walked over to the man. "The next time I tell you to hit the ground running," Bolan said, "I hope you've got the sense to listen to me."

Renfrow shrugged resignedly. "When you're right, you're right," he said.

"Go get those cuts taken care of," Bolan said.

The man nodded, moving off into the confusion of the roadway.

Bolan walked back to the Mercedes, closing the driver's side door. The performance of the vehicle had been poor at best. He'd have to either find a way to modify the armor or beef up the engine. He watched as Trevans and the phony Senator Torrance emerged from the woods, Trevans scowling in his direction.

General Abrams from the DIA removed himself from a small group of Pentagon brass and walked over. "We've got a long way to go, don't we?"

"Yeah, I'm afraid so," Bolan answered.

Abrams took a long breath. "Well, it's a start," he said, as if to convince himself. "I believe these gentlemen will want you to say a few words. Maybe you can mix the good with the bad, eh?"

"I'm not much of a politician," Bolan said.

"Just do your best," Abrams said gruffly, then turned and walked off.

Bolan frowned as he climbed onto the trunk of the Mercedes. "Can I have your attention please," he said. "Gather around."

He watched as the group of about forty men formed a semicircle around him. "What we've seen today is a demonstration of counterterrorist methods. Although the target, in this case Senator Torrance, was saved, the operation was far from successful. The biggest problem I've had in training Secret Servicemen is overcoming their natural tendency to not take the job seriously. They are all highly trained professionals who know their jobs and have performed them successfully, in some cases for many years.

"What they don't understand, what most people don't understand, is that today's wave of terrorism is unlike anything they've been exposed to. In most cases with typical bodyguard protection, the simple presence of the bodyguard is enough to drive away the rational man. But terrorists are not rational. They are highly motivated individuals, absolutely prepared to die to advance their cause, however strange or incredible that cause may seem to us. Bodyguards mean nothing to them except more targets, a large body count for the television cameras. They expect a dirty fight. They look forward to a dirty fight so they may, in turn, die with honor."

Bolan watched the faces watching him. Most were blank, unreadable. He wasn't sure he was getting through. "My men behaved with inexcusable laxity this afternoon. They failed to take the threat seriously. I was surprised from the rear because my man in back wasn't doing his job. My man in the front seat had effectively taken himself out of the action by laying his weapon out of easy reach and letting his mind wander from the task at hand. And this, gentlemen, was when we knew, *knew,* that we were coming under attack sometime during the trip.

''I was disappointed at the lack of attentiveness. I was disappointed at the slow reactions once the danger became real. These men would not have survived a well-coordinated terrorist attack. The entire carload of bodyguards would be dead right now, and a candidate for the presidency would either be held hostage or lying in a ditch with a bullet in his brain. Think about it.''

Bolan jumped to the ground and walked away from the grumbling crowd. He had known they wouldn't like what he had to say, but worse than that, he feared they wouldn't take it seriously.

He climbed behind the wheel of the Mercedes and closed the door. He watched through the rearview mirror as an olive-drab wrecker hooked up to the limo blocking the road, preparing to drag it away. Good. He was ready to make the trip back to Andrews Air Force Base where this fiasco had started, and he was ready to make it alone.

He started the engine, then noticed a piece of paper on the passenger seat. He picked it up.

CALL BROGNOLA, STAT.

Hal, his friend at Justice who had stuck with him, even during the lean years. The man who had brought him back into the fold. Something was up. Finally. He hoped his training days were at an end.

He put the car in reverse, but a hand reached through the front window and grabbed his arm before he backed up. Trevans was looking at him with fierce eyes.

"You're a son of a bitch, you know that? You just ranked my whole squad in front of a lot of brass."

"Your men are lax," Bolan replied, jerking his arm from Trevans's grasp. "They're going to have to learn if they want to stay alive."

Trevans spoke low, through clenched teeth. "I won't forget this, you bastard," he hissed. "I'm going to get you somehow."

"You take that to the bank," Bolan said. "See what you can borrow on it." He hit the gas, spinning the man away from the car, and backed slowly into the now thinning crowd.

2

Blocker smiled at the vaguely Oriental-looking woman who worked the posh registration desk, taking in her brown eyes, trying to melt her with his own. "It sure must be exciting working here in Hollywood," he told her. "Do you get a lot of famous movie stars in here?"

She smiled, looking down demurely to break the embarrassing eye contact. "Paul Newman came in once...with his wife," she said, her eyes stealing up to see if he was still watching her. "He was smaller than I thought, but so-o-o handsome."

"Gosh," the man said. "We sure don't have anything like this back in Fort Worth. Me and my family are going to the taping of Johnny's show tonight."

"That should be fun," the young woman responded.

"Yeah. Do you think I could have an extra room key for the kids?" he asked. "Sometimes they like to go the opposite direction of the old folks."

"Certainly, Mr...."

"Masters," the man said. "Farley Masters."

The woman got another key from the beehive behind the desk and handed it to him, their fingers lingering an extra second before the contact was broken. "Enjoy yourself, Mr. Masters," she said.

"Call me Farley," the man replied, his eyes falling to her name tag. "And you're...Odette."

She smiled, nodding.

"Could I ask you for a big favor, Odette?" Blocker asked. "I've got some clothes in your laundry here, and they tell me they won't be ready until noon tomorrow. Now, we've got to take an early checkout to get back on the road for Texas. Isn't there some way you maybe could put in a good word and hurry them along?"

She frowned for a second. "I really don't have any control over..."

He fixed her with his eyes again, oozing sincerity. "Please?" he said in a small voice. "It's real important."

She fought an internal battle for a second, then physically slumped a touch. "I'll see what I can do," she promised.

"Thanks, Odette," he said gratefully, and reached across the counter to take her hand. "You've made my day." He brought her hand to his lips and kissed it gently. "Do you have to work all night around this place? When in the world do they let you get some sleep?"

She smiled with a theatrical toss of her head. "I only have to work until midnight."

"The witching hour," he said, then winked. "Maybe I'll see you later."

"Maybe," she returned.

He held up the key. "Thanks again," he said, pocketing it. He turned from the registration desk of the Sunset Hyatt and walked across the long, narrow lobby and out the front doors into the Los Angeles dusk. He'd use the woman later to solidify an alibi.

He thought about how strange people were, how quick they were to accept friendship and intimacy from someone they didn't know, especially if the stranger was physically appealing. For someone willing to work with the basically gullible nature of his fellow man, much could be accomplished in life.

The rest of his team was waiting for him by the hotel drive-up—the Masters family of Fort Worth, Texas, originally from Abilene. Wife Loreen, petite and red-haired, seventeen-year-old Mary Ann, pretty and a touch wild, sixteen-year-old Jeff, lean and rugged like his daddy.

For all intents and purposes, they *were* the Masters family. The names had been carefully gleaned from cemetery headstones, a family killed in a car wreck ten years previously whose birth ages matched up with the team's closely. After finding suitable dead people, they simply went to the bureau of vital statistics and said they'd lost their identifications in a house fire, at which point they were all issued new birth certificates. From there they built a life, quickly and quietly. A home was purchased in Fort Worth, "lost" driver's licenses were reissued from the birth certificates, phony work and school records were inserted in the proper places through trial and error access to the right computer networks. The tentacles branched out, as credit cards and passports were issued from all the other information, and within the space of a month, the Masters had managed to build a phony life as complete and fulfilling as any ever experienced by a "real" family.

Now they could get down to business.

"Did you get the extra key?" Loreen asked as he approached, no trace of an Irish accent evident in her studied Midwestern speech.

He took out the key and handed it to her. "Don't do anything to call attention to yourself," he said coldly.

Her green eyes didn't waver as she looked up at him. "I can take care of myself," she said.

He nodded. "I know."

"Here comes the car," Jeff said as the valet pulled up in their innocuous Ford, which he'd retrieved from the back parking lot. "How about me driving?"

"Jeff got to drive last time," Mary Ann said, pouting. "It's my turn."

"You've never driven in a combat situation," Jeff responded, glaring at her.

"Listen to Mr. Loudmouth!" Mary Ann said. "How about blabbing to the whole world—"

"Stop it!" Blocker said in low tones. "Both of you. I'm driving tonight. And if you don't curb it, Jeff, I'll curb it for you."

The boy, whose real name was Christian Flemming, took a breath and cast his gaze downward. "Yes, sir," he said quietly. They would all use the names they had adopted coming into the country for consistency's sake. Never would they utter their real names.

The valet squealed to a stop right beside them and climbed out, smiling. "Here you are, Mr. Masters."

"Thanks, Bob," the man said, giving the valet a five-dollar tip. "We'll say hello to Johnny Carson for you tonight."

"You do that," the man returned, smiling at the tip.

They climbed into the car, Loreen in the front passenger seat, the two teenagers in the back, and the man slid the medium-sized sedan into the evening rush along the Sunset Strip. The hotel was located at the junction of La Cienega Boulevard and Sunset, just on the edge of Beverly Hills and at the base of the West Hollywood hills, where magnificent homes loomed over the edge of the canyons, and the movie people, the American royalty, held sway over their dominion.

Sunset Strip was the gaudy kingdom of the kings and queens of glitz. Alight with neon and flashy billboards advertising recent movies, it was mostly a meat market of prepubescent hookers of both sexes and a restaurant district for L.A.'s large homosexual population. This was what the extra key was for. Loreen would celebrate the success of their job tonight among the slime.

To Blocker it was nothing but a stretch of good road with multiple escape routes. In a city with a place like Sunset Strip as its heart, nothing was impossible. To do his business here, among the craziness, was going to be almost too easy. He made a mental note to have either Mary Ann or Jeff watch *The Tonight Show* and report on its contents.

He drove east two blocks past the hotel, turned left at a hamburger restaurant that was a converted railroad dining car and started up the steep canyon drive that took them immediately into the royal domain. He would visit a king tonight; it would be a visit that, he hoped, all of America would remember.

"Wexler should be the next one," Loreen said, her eyes fixed on the roadway and the route they had practiced earlier that day. In the back seat, Jeff and Mary Ann bickered constantly, the usual teenage sibling rivalry. Blocker accepted it as hormonal, knowing they wouldn't let him down in a pinch.

He had purchased them, at ages two and three, in Vietnam in 1973 for two thousand dollars and a jeep. Brother and sister, they had been taken alive when their missionary parents hadn't been quick enough to avoid advancing North Vietnamese armies during their final sweep through the south near the end of the war. He had raised and trained them himself in his compound in the demilitarized zone of Paraguay. He trusted their instincts as he trusted his own.

"Get out the ordnance," he called over his shoulder. The teenagers fell silent immediately and tore out the back seat of the rental car, revealing a cache of weapons and ammo. Compact Ingram MAC-10 SMGs with shoulder straps were passed around, as well as extra clips. The electrician's case went to Blocker. No one spoke as they geared up for the mission, Jeff taking out the coveralls and ski masks that would prevent witnesses from giving their descriptions to the authorities.

Blocker turned onto Wexler, the road winding ever upward. The man they were going to visit was important royalty, his house near the top of the hill.

They pulled alongside a high wall that was a half block from the big front gates of the estate. When

Blocker got out with his electrician's kit, Loreen slid over to the driver's seat. Loreen, aka Cory Moran, had been doing demolition work for the IRA and had been involved in the explosion that had killed Lord Mountbatten. She'd been free-lancing for Blocker for the past few years. She was a cool customer, but Blocker chose her for this mission because she had been a successful IRA fund-raiser in the United States and knew her way around.

A streetlight attached to a telephone pole bathed the entire area in blue-green light. Blocker closed his door, then leaned through the open windows. "Jeff," he said, "take care of that light, would you?"

"Sure thing, Dad," Jeff said, climbing out of the back, a slingshot in hand.

Blocker watched as Jeff took a handful of marbles out of his pocket, then he looked up and down the street to make sure it was clear, not stopping to appreciate the truly incredible view of downtown Los Angeles afforded from this height before walking toward the gate.

He hadn't gone ten feet before he heard a slight snap, followed by glass breaking as the streetlight died in a haze of its own vapor, plunging that section of the road into darkness.

Blocker made the gate. It was iron, electronically sealed, with a closed-circuit television camera keeping watch over the area. A Private Property sign was affixed to the gate.

The terrorist stooped, put his case on the ground and opened it. He pulled out a small, powerful transmitter, turned it on and stuck it onto the wall beside the gate. Its pattern would set up a healthy feedback with the gate TV, effectively jamming it out.

Then he did a quick study of the gate. Its seal was good, a static charge that held the bars would set off an alarm if anyone tried to force the seal. It could be a highly effective deterrent *if* the person trying to break in didn't know the physics behind the workings of the device.

Blocker took the hand-held electromagnet out of his case and turned it on to a low-level hum, running it up and down the seal of the gate until he found the point of electron bonding. Then he reversed the magnet's polarity, and the barrier sprung open soundlessly. He pushed both sides all the way open with the backs of his hands, then stepped quickly back to the street, flashing a penlight twice in the direction of the car. Loreen immediately turned on the engine and drove the vehicle—without lights—through the front gates. Blocker closed them behind her.

Blocker waved the Ford off the driveway just inside the gate, the team jumping out quickly and getting into their coveralls and masks. The house, fifty yards from the gate, sat in a yard heavily planted with trees and shrubs. It had been constructed to one side of the large lot so that its owners would have a spectacular view of the Hollywood vista.

Blocker looked at his watch. He wanted to be in and out of there within thirty minutes. Given the seclusion of the grounds, there shouldn't be any problem with noise. The man they were about to hit was John Seales, a movie producer who had won an Oscar the year before for a film about U.S. involvement in Central America. He was married to a fast-rising starlet who had won fame in a James Bond movie and as a Southern belle in a Civil War picture. Blocker never went to the movies, so he didn't see any sense in them.

Loreen passed around an aerosol can of medicated first-aid spray that they used on their fingers to obliterate their prints. Jeff threw the empty can and the electrician's case back into the vehicle, then each slung a stuttergun over a shoulder.

"Jeff, the phone lines," Blocker said, slipping into his knit cap. "Mary Ann, the surveillance and alarm equipment on the electric pole. And just get that stuff. I want to be able to see in there. Loreen, the caretaker's house sits off a bit behind the main house. Use your K-Bar, okay?"

Loreen smiled, pulling out her knife from one of her stylish boots.

"Okay, go! Rendezvous at the front door in ten minutes."

They all turned and scurried off silently, Blocker moving casually toward the house, passing the Sealeses' carport on the way, their three cars nestled in their berths for the night. There was a red Mercedes sports car parked in front of the house. Visitors, but no more than two. No problem.

He wandered around the house. There was a stable in the back, several horses standing quietly in a small pasture, but no dogs. He moved to the side of the house and saw lights, then approached the window to take a quick look.

A small crack between the draperies afforded him a view. Four people were sitting on a long couch, watching a movie on a big-screen TV. Most of the lights were out, but enough were on for Blocker to identify his marks. He made Seales and his wife. The other man was older, a movie star from the past who even Blocker recognized. The fourth person was a young blond woman wearing an extremely low-cut sweater.

He pulled back from the window, glanced up and saw Mary Ann at work on the high electric pole. Walking to the back, he found a door with a screen, which he quietly opened. He wrapped baling wire around the door handle, closed the screen door on the wire and wrapped a length around the outside handle. No way would anyone be able to open the back door from the inside.

He looked at his watch. Eight minutes had passed. He moved to the front of the building for the meet. The house was nice, Blocker thought, a Southern antebellum style so much more durable and stylish than the gaudy mishmash of styles he had seen through most of the Hollywood Hills, all lumped under the heading of "modern."

Jeff was already there when he arrived, the boy's ski mask pulled down over his face revealing only his excited eyes. Blocker could see what he was thinking.

"No sex this time, okay?" he said, and it wasn't a question. "We don't want to confuse the issue."

"But, Dad..."

"You'll be able to buy all you want when this is over. Just business tonight."

Jeff nodded, masking his disappointment with an exaggerated visual check of his small machine gun.

Mary Ann ran up to them, tucking her long hair under the mask. Loreen sauntered casually behind her, wiping the bloody blade of the K-Bar on her coveralls.

"Any problems?" Blocker asked her.

Loreen smiled widely and put on a highly stylized Southern accent. "Why Ah told you Ah could take care of mahself, Farley honey."

Blocker looked at them. "This one shouldn't be any problem, but it'll get us all the publicity we can handle. Don't tarry, and don't take anything. We're being well paid."

He bent with his number four pick and went to work on the front door, the ten-foot oak slab springing open easily. As they unslung their weapons, they could hear music and laughter coming from the back of the house. Blocker looked at the teenagers. "Search the place," he said. "Take care of any problems."

Loreen gripped his arm tightly in her excitement. They lived for the missions, all of them. Next to this, the rest of life was a waste of time. He pulled the mask down over his face.

"Let's go," he whispered, and they moved quickly into the house, Jeff hurrying up the stairs as Mary Ann ran off toward the darkened dining room area. In the formal living room, Blocker noticed a large fireplace where they could burn the coveralls when they were through. He and Loreen charged toward the sounds in the den, breaking quickly into the large room. Startled, the four people jumped up from the couch that sat in a pit in the center.

"Sit down!" Blocker ordered, and when they weren't quick to comply, he fired a short burst into the TV, which sparked loudly, then died. "Lights!" he yelled to Loreen.

"Where are they?" she called in the near darkness.

"Nobody move!" Blocker yelled. A second later three of their quarry had scattered around the room. The blonde had raced from the room. He could hear her pulling desperately at the back door.

"Sit down!" Blocker yelled again.

"Now listen," said the old actor, a rugged type from adventure films. He moved toward Blocker. "I don't know who you people are, but—"

He never got to finish. Blocker laced his midsection with a 9 mm burst from ten feet away. The man fell backward to the carpet, struggling to a kneeling position. He uttered a piercing scream when he realized his insides were all over his hands. Then he pitched forward, dead before he hit the floor.

"Now will you sit down?" Blocker asked quietly.

Seales's wife began to scream, her hands cradling her head as she stared at the body.

"My God!" Seales yelled, his face pale. "You've shot him, you've—"

"Sit down, Mr. Seales," Blocker said calmly, watching as Mary Ann brought the blonde back into the room. "And stuff a rag into your wife's mouth if you know what's good for her."

Seales's lips moved silently as he pulled his wife down on the sofa with him, bringing her head to his chest to muffle her sobs. He looked drained, beaten.

'If it's ransom," the man said, "we've got—"

"Quiet," Blocker ordered, placing a finger against his ski-masked lips. "Please."

Mary Ann brought the blonde to the sofa, the woman gagging when she saw the body. She turned her head from the sight and breathed quickly, panting as the words came tumbling from her lips. "Look, I don't belong here. I don't even know these people. I just thought it'd be . . . you know, good for my career to meet . . . to meet—"

"Please be quiet," Blocker said.

"I don't care what you do to them," the woman said frantically. "I haven't seen your faces. I can't identify . . . identify any of you. I'll walk . . . home. I can walk. Nobody even knows I'm here, I—"

Blocker put up a hand. "That won't be necessary."

The woman's eyes widened. "What about me? Do you want me? Do anything you want . . . I can make you feel good, I—"

"It's all right," Blocker soothed. "Nobody's going to hurt you. Mary Ann will take care of you."

"Don't you worry," Mary Ann said sweetly, and moved up beside the woman. With a smooth motion, she jammed the machine gun into the woman's ribs and pulled the trigger, the blast literally throwing the blonde across the room and up against a wall. She fell to the ground, her eyes still wide, her lips spewing blood bubbles.

Seales's wife screamed again, her body shaking uncontrollably.

"What do you want?" Seales yelled. "God in heaven, what do you want?"

"I bring you greetings from the colonel," Blocker said, and watched as the man's face blanked for several seconds. Then slowly, like the change from dusk to dark, a growing look of horror transformed the man's features into a strained, ugly mask.

"Dear God," he whispered, pulling his wife to him again.

"You have a nice place here," Blocker observed, looking around at the expensive, overstuffed furniture and the original movie posters that hung in silver frames on the wall. "You must do quite well in the motion picture business. Funny what people will spend their money on. Never really understood the average person's sensibilities, myself."

He shrugged when Seales didn't answer, then walked over to the large wet bar. A videotape camera sat on a tripod next to it. "What's this?" Blocker asked, not expecting an answer. "Does this make movies?"

Seales just stared at him, his eyes lost in some faraway haze, his wife totally out of touch beside him, inhuman sounds issuing from her trembling lips.

Blocker stared hard at him. "I asked you a question."

"Y-yes," Seales stammered. "I-it makes movies."

"How?"

"It's n-not hard, you—"

"Come show me."

Seales hurried to comply, his wife screaming loudly when he moved away from her.

"Shut up, you stupid bitch!" Loreen yelled, running over to shake her.

The woman slumped over on the couch, her eyes dark and staring.

"Wh-what do you want to do?" Seales asked, his hands shaking as he moved the tripod into the center of the floor.

"The room," Blocker said, gesturing. "Your wife...can we take a picture of your wife?"

Seales nodded, setting up the camera and juicing it to life. He indicated that Blocker should look through the viewfinder.

Blocker bent to peer through the viewer, which showed a large section of the room, the woman on the sofa in the center. "Excellent," he said. "Can this thing run without anyone working it?"

Seales nodded, flipping on the automatic switch. The camera whirred to life. "Listen," Seales said, "whatever he's paying you, I can do better, I can—"

"Don't insult me, Mr. Seales," Blocker said, interrupting. "I'm an honest businessman. How long could I stay in business if I dishonored my commitments? Please go and sit down. Your wife needs your assistance."

"I beg you, don't hurt my wife. She doesn't know anything about this."

Blocker smiled. "I won't," he said.

The man went back to the couch. His wife had lapsed into near catatonia, her body limp as Seales tried to comfort her.

Blocker smiled at Loreen and pointed to the camera. She nodded broadly in agreement. Blocker had been searching for just the right way in which to take credit for tonight, and the technocratic world was providing the perfect impetus in the form of the videocamera. He couldn't have asked for better.

"Look what I found!" Jeff yelled excitedly, literally dragging a woman in a nightgown into the room and pushing her to the floor. She seemed to be about twenty years old and was whimpering loudly, guttural sounds issuing from her lips. Her presence snapped Seales's wife out of her trance immediately.

"No-o-o!" she screamed, trying to jump up, Seales himself halfway across the room. "That's my sister, please!"

"Enough!" Blocker said, bringing up the MAC-10 as Jeff pulled the young woman to her feet. "Another step and the girl dies."

The room became quiet.

"What's the matter, sweetheart?" Jeff asked the woman as he rubbed a hand all over her face and hair. "Cat got your tongue?"

"Please don't hurt her," Seales said. "She's retarded. Sh-she can't talk."

Blocker smiled. "Now sit back down. We're all nearly finished here. If you cooperate, nothing will happen to your sister... What's her name?"

"Beth," the woman said quietly.

"Nothing will happen to Beth," Blocker said. "But you must cooperate."

"I'll do anything," the woman said.

"Good. Sit back down."

The camera still whirred as the Sealeses took their places on the couch. Blocker walked back behind the camera to look through the viewfinder. "Jeff," he said, "you move over by the couch with the girl.

That's right. Now, you other two stand behind our happy couple." The women moved to comply, the shot lining up nicely in the viewfinder. "Good."

Blocker moved from behind the camera, strutting up to his players, acting very much the director. "First, I'm going to make a small speech," he said, "then we'll begin. So. The camera's rolling and—how do you say it in show business?—action!"

Blocker turned to the camera, staring straight into its unblinking eye. "People of America. To you and your great Satan president, I am here to tell you that it is time to pay for the sins that you have perpetrated against the Islamic peoples of the world."

He pointed to the sofa, to Seales. "This man is an enemy of Islam, and of a Palestinian homeland, and he is paying the price of the infidel. So are all of you, our enemies. You have bombed our cities and supported the Jewish dogs who took our homes from us. Now, we bring that war back to you. Now, we fight on *your* ground, in *your* homes."

He moved in closer to the camera, his gaze never wavering. "In the name of the great North African Republic, the just vengeance of Allah be upon all of you. Only blood will purge your sins. John Seales knows. The others on my list know. And no matter what you do, no matter how much you pray and how much action you take, you will not be able to stop us. We are vengeance, and we are coming for you next."

He turned to stare at Jeff. "Kill the girl," he said.

3

Bolan sat, his stomach tightened to a hard ball, and watched as the ski-masked man on the television brought up his SMG and blew off the retarded girl's head, laughing as he pushed the still-writhing body onto the lap of her hysterical sister.

He had watched the tape three times, the horror and revulsion he felt growing stronger with each viewing until he wanted to reach into the TV screen with his bare hands and somehow obliterate the magnetic vibrations that made the pictures and in so doing end the nightmare that they portrayed. It made him feel dirty to even be a part of the same species that could conceive of such evil.

He was the only one in Brognola's office. The others had left, faces pale, after the first viewing. But he had stayed, rewinding the film with an unsteady hand to watch it again, and again. He had focused on the leader's eyes.

After the killing of the girl, Seales had tried to jump them, but one of the women had responded by shooting his legs and then, after he had fallen, his arms. He was forced to lay there helplessly screaming as his wife's throat was cut. It took her several minutes to die, and by the time she had, Seales had left whatever humanity he possessed far behind and had been reduced to a gurgling, mindless creature. And that was a blessing.

They killed him then, too—slowly, by degrees; but in a macabre sense it was simply gilding the lily. There had been no more satisfaction to be had out of John Seales.

Bolan sat up, watching intently. This was the part he kept coming back for, the reason he had watched the tape three times. The leader of the group came up close to the camera, staring into it intently.

"There, you see," he said. "This is how we treat the enemies of Islam and the great leader Moammar Khaddafi. We will kill again, and you won't be able to stop us. You are not safe on your streets. You are not safe in your houses. Do everything you can, but in two days, more will die."

Bolan moved quickly to the portable television that sat on Hal's desk and hit the Pause button on the VCR. Frozen in time was a close-up of the man's eyes, the screen burning with his eyes. There was no passion in them, no bloodlust, no righteous indignation. They were simply two lumps of dark ice, frozen and deadly.

The man was a professional; the Executioner was convinced of it.

He had seen enough. He shut off the equipment and crossed the carpeted floor to the office door and threw it open.

Hal, looking old and tired, sat on the edge of his secretary's desk. Anyone who had watched the horror of that videotape would look old and tired. Bolan nodded to him once, then walked back into the office.

Hal went in behind him, closing the door and moving to sit behind his desk. "I sent the others on," he said, then picked up the coffee cup that sat amid the clutter. He frowned at its contents, but took a drink anyway.

"Why?" Bolan asked, leaning against the desktop on stiff arms. "Don't you think the man meant what he said on the tape?"

"I don't know the answer to that, Striker," Hal answered, and Bolan didn't believe it for a minute. "It's just not really in our jurisdiction."

"Justice just doesn't want to pursue it, that's all." Bolan walked back to the small sofa that sat by the window overlooking the Washington Monument. "So what happens now?"

"The LAPD's working with it. Maybe the FBI can put a foot in there someplace."

"Hell..."

Brognola slammed a hand down on the desk angrily, several papers flying off to float groundward. "Look at the facts. The people involved spoke perfect English without foreign accents. The LA cops think that the terrorist angle might just have been put in there to throw everybody off the track. Movie people make a lot of enemies. It could have been some crazy actor's revenge, or even be connected up with some kind of drug deal or something. Who knows, maybe even the Mafia..."

"The Mafia takes care of things quickly and quietly," Bolan said. "They wouldn't go to all the trouble to advertise it. Good God, Hal. These people made dupes of that tape and left them at every television station in Los Angeles. The whole world has seen this sickness by now.''

''Maybe a crazy serial killer,'' Brognola suggested, trying the cold coffee again and getting the same bitter results. ''You know, they gave credit to Khaddafi, but the colonel has been screaming his denial ever since, saying he'll take care of the killers himself when they're caught. I mean, if your theory is right, what possible connection could this man have with the Libyan government? He's been in Hollywood making movies for the past fifteen years.''

Bolan leaned forward, staring at Brognola with cold eyes. ''Listen, Hal. Every act we saw on that TV screen was calculated to create a desired effect. The people who committed these murders were pros hired to do a terrorist job, and like all terrorist jobs, the proper credit was given so the people of this country would know who to be afraid of. I don't care what Khaddafi says. He's never told the truth before. I know a hundred people like the son of a bitch on that tape, and any one of them could have done the same job. We're looking at professional terrorism on American shores. If this were Europe—''

Brognola put up a hand. ''I know, the SAS would be in on it. But that's just the problem, isn't it? This country doesn't have a 'sanctioned' antiterrorist unit like the SAS.'' The man stood and stretched. Bolan felt sorry for him. He was trying hard to work within the system and still accomplish something. In his quiet, *legal* way, Hal Brognola had probably done as much as the Executioner to stem the rising tide of organized crime and terrorism that threatened to swamp America. It was simply not enough, would never be enough.

"That's our problem, isn't it?" Hal continued. "We've got no legal arm to conduct investigations into this sort of thing. Nobody wants to believe that it's possible, so until their noses get rubbed in it, they'll never believe it. Hell, Striker, I don't want to believe it myself."

Bolan pointed to the television. "You want to watch it again? I'll convince you."

Brognola waved it off. He sat down again. "What do you want from me?"

"I want to go after this guy, Hal," Bolan said with intensity. "I want to send his head back to Tripoli in a box. I've seen his kind before, know how his mind works. I can track him, stop him before he pulls anything else."

"You have other responsibilities."

"Nothing's more important than this."

Brognola sighed and stared once more at his coffee cup. This time, however, he left it alone. "What about Jake Torrance?" he asked.

"The senator? What about him?"

"He phoned earlier and is asking for beefed-up security protection. Says he's had some threats. He's especially asked that you be assigned to protect him."

"Guess he liked my demonstration," Bolan replied. "But he doesn't need me. He's already got protection. I'd be a fifth wheel."

Brognola thought for a time, then began to write on a sheet of yellow legal paper. "The most we can hope for is a call for cooperation with the Los Angeles Police, if pushed to it," he said at last. "We'll send you out as a special representative of the President, just an overseer actually. You'll have no power or jurisdiction, but at least we should be able to get them to share the results of their investigation with you."

"That's it?"

"Best we can do for now. You've gone out with less." Hal tore off the sheet of paper and handed it to Bolan.

"Thanks," Bolan said, folding the paper into his pocket.

Hal nodded. "Now that we're setting up the file on this, we're going to have to call it something. Any ideas?"

Bolan thought of the man's eyes. "Freon," he said. "Call it Project Freon."

Hal wrote the name down, then dropped the pen, rubbing his eyes with the heels of his hands. "Those people who died," he said, "were household names all over this country. Feelings about this are running high, and the people involved with the investigation are going to be under intense pressure. You're walking into a crucible, Striker, as a government representative. This is the biggest thing to hit this country since the Charles Manson, Tate-LaBianca killings. Exercise a little discretion, okay?"

Bolan walked to the door. "I don't care about the pressures, Hal," he said, "or the politics of the situation. I'm watching professional terrorism gain a foothold in this country, and I'm going to do something about it. If you don't want to back me on this, I'll do it on my own. But you're not going to restrict me in any way, shape or form.''

''You're a tough man to do business with,'' Hal grunted.

''But you love me anyway,'' Bolan replied, opening the door.

Brognola snorted his amusement. ''Give 'em hell.''

''Message received,'' Bolan said, and left, closing the door behind him.

He moved through the huge plethora of Justice Department offices, leaving his ''Mike Belasko'' identification badge with the security people on his way out of the building.

It wasn't until he had guided his Porsche onto the Baltimore-Washington Parkway and got the speed up to a decent pace that he gave some deep thought to his mission. No one, not even Hal, appreciated what was happening the way he did.

If his quarry had set up merely a passable cover, if he was only half as smart as he seemed to be, he could easily move anywhere at all, killing with impunity anyone he wanted. The man with the Freon eyes could single-handedly throw America into a state of paranoia unparalleled in its history.

Fear is the air and lifeblood to a terrorist. A successful campaign of fear would open the door to a large-scale American terrorist war waged from the Middle East. Success breeds more success, as evidenced by the French, who thought they could appease terrorism and instead were ground into the dust.

The only real hope that Bolan felt he had lay in something Freon had said. He referred to people on a "list." Everything the man had said was calculated, so the mention of a list was certainly not spontaneous. Random killings cannot be predicted nor defended against. But the list suggested motivation. It made absolutely no sense to Bolan, but there it was. If there was, indeed, a list of victims, the list would have an intelligence and motivation behind it that could, in turn, be investigated and ferreted out. That's what the Executioner intended to do.

How could movie executive John Seales be on a terrorist hit list? It didn't figure. Maybe he had made a film that had angered Khaddafi. But, by the same token, a great many people did things that angered Khaddafi. If the colonel was looking for enemies, he could start with the telephone directories of every city in the United States. No, this smacked of something personal, something that offended the Libyan leader's sense of honor. But what?

The possibility of error in his approach never occurred to Bolan. The entire world could tell him he was on the wrong track and it wouldn't matter to him, for he had seen those eyes on the videotape, the eyes of a mercenary who didn't care who handed out the paycheck. The eyes belonged to a man meticulous in all things, especially in protecting his own life. He would be tough opposition—the toughest.

Bolan was staying at a hotel near the renovated harbor area of downtown Baltimore, if for no other reason than to catch a whiff of exuberance in the heady mix of salty sea air and pungent odors from the

McCormick Spice Company on the waterfront. It was late afternoon by the time he arrived back at his hotel and made reservations for an evening flight to L.A.

He packed his bag, then slipped into the combat harness that cradled Big Thunder and the Beretta 93 R and as he glanced around the room one last time to see if he had forgotten anything, there was a knock on the door.

He moved quietly across the shag carpet to look through the eye level peephole that gave a view of the hall. A young woman, in her early twenties at best, stood casually outside the door, an overnight bag hanging from her shoulder. Her hands were in the open.

He slid the Beretta from the leather shoulder holster and held it in his left hand, out of sight, as he opened the door a crack with his right.

"I think you've got the wrong room," he said.

Her eyes narrowed, and she looked at the number on the door again. "Are you Mack Bolan?" she asked.

He shook his head. "Sorry, you've got the wrong room." He tried to close the door, but she jammed her foot in the opening.

"Project Freon," she said, and pushed a note through the crack.

He took the note, but didn't open the door.

Mack,
Knew you'd be uncooperative if I told you back at State, but on deals like this we have to send technical help along with our investigator.

The operative you're looking at is Joan Meredith. Don't let her looks fool you. Besides being a computer whiz and brilliant cryptographer, she had early training with LAPD and can probably help you in that regard.

So don't give her a hard time. Get to work.

A friend

Bolan opened the door and let her enter, closing the door behind her. "I don't need you," he said. "I have no intention of working with you. Go back and tell Hal thanks, but no thanks."

"That's what he said you'd say. And he told me your cover name is Mike Belasko," she replied.

He stared at her. She couldn't have been over five foot three, and her short hair and upturned nose made her look like everybody's idea of a twelve-year-old tomboy. "I can handle this by myself."

"He told me you'd say that, too."

Bolan looked at his watch. "I've got a plane to catch, lady. Why don't you go on and do...whatever it is that you do."

"Fine," she replied. "Since I'm on the same plane and involved in the same investigation, I suppose we'll see each other from time to time. I hope you don't get in my way or mess anything up."

"Don't you get it, lady?"

"Joan."

"This is dangerous. I don't need you getting in my way or getting hurt."

She stared at him. "Listen, jerk," she said, angered. "I was busting junkies in Watts when I was twenty-one years old. At twenty-two I shot it out with three syndicate men without backup. I'm an ex-judo instructor, an expert on weapons and ballistics, computers and electronics. I speak three languages, excluding English, and am a fair to middling anthropologist. So don't give me any of this 'little woman' crap. I've got my orders and I intend to carry them out, with or without your blessing."

Bolan smiled slightly. Feisty. He liked that. He'd give her a chance. "Got your car here?" he asked.

She nodded.

"Okay. We'll ride to the airport together. We'll talk about what kind of cooperation we can expect from the Los Angeles Police Department."

Patricia Blackman stood on the wide slatted porch of the plush ranch house and stared out across the dark vista of open New Mexico desert that stretched as far as she could see. She wasn't much on this rustic crap, but after watching Johnny Seales get his guts ripped apart on national television, she was willing to put up with the desolation for a while.

Maybe she could even get some mileage out of it for herself. She could see the banner on the cover: "*You* Magazine Publisher Goes Native," or something like that. Pat had always believed that her success in the publishing business had been partially due to the fact that she publicized her own life and times along with the multitude of celebrities, writers and politicians who filled the large photographed pages of her magazine. She had made *You* and herself American institutions at the same time. Quite a success story for little Patty Blakowski from Queens, a dream come true—although John's death was too much a reminder of the real nature of her success...

The phone was ringing inside the huge house. One of the servants would answer it. When she had called her rich gentleman friend who was touring Europe and asked if he had a place where she could "get away for a few days," little did she realize that she'd end up in the Western New Mexico version of the palace at Versailles.

The night was coming up chill, but beautiful, with a star field far larger than anything she could see around the city lights of New York. There was a main gate a couple of hundred yards distant, which was now being manned by her bodyguards from the front seats of a four-wheel-drive Bronco. Other security people, ten in all, prowled the grounds looking for an excuse to earn the huge salary and expenses they were getting paid. No, Pat Blackman hadn't come all this way in life to get sliced up by some madman with a long memory. She'd survive this, and survive it in style.

She heard the door open behind her and turned to see Maria, the live-in housekeeper, staring at her. "Someone for you on the phone," the woman said tonelessly.

"Who is it?" Pat asked.

"A man. He said he was returning your call."

She nodded and moved into the house, the rich lacquered knotty pine of the walls shining warmly under the house lights. The place rambled in all directions, but Pat had already claimed the den as her spot. It was a masculine place, full of overstuffed furniture and hand-carved humidors, and it made her feel somehow safer.

She sat on the oxblood leather couch and stretched out a denim-clad leg, resting it on the wagon wheel coffee table. Then she picked up the receiver of the old-style black telephone off the end table and brought it to her ear. She was feeling suddenly nervous.

"Hello?"

"Patty?" She hadn't heard that voice since 1969, nearly two decades ago, but she recognized it instantly, as if it had been with her all the while. The thought made her even more nervous.

"D-did you hear about John?" she asked. "Did you see what they—"

"Yes, I saw," came the reply. "Now don't panic. This may not mean anything."

"Is that what you think, that it doesn't mean anything?" she asked, feeling angry and wondering why.

It took a few seconds before her answer came. "No, I don't think so. Are you taking precautions?"

"You bet I am," Pat said. "No one but the man who lent me this place knows where it is, and *he's* out of the country. My executive secretary has the phone number, and you have the phone number, but that's it."

"Good. The people who killed Johnny can't stay free forever. They'll get caught...they have to be. Meantime, I've doubled my own security."

"Easy for you," she said, then laughed shortly. "You don't have to pay for it."

"You have to pay for everything in life, Patty," the voice said with melancholy.

"You got that right." She felt herself softening, realizing finally why she had called him at all. "How have you been?" she asked in a small voice, remembering a relationship that had felt so right but that had never held together because of greed and twisting fortunes.

"I've been okay," came the answer, just as soft. The years couldn't suffocate the memories. No wonder they had avoided each other all this time. "I read about you in your magazine. You...never married."

"Neither did you," she heard herself say, and so many feelings were tumbling out, threatening to drown her and the carefully constructed life she had led for so long. "I—I sometimes like to think that it's my fault."

"It is. I guess when a person sells his soul—"

"No!" she said harshly. "I've thought about that for nearly twenty years. Let's think of tomorrow. Maybe...maybe when this is all over..."

"Yeah, maybe. Look out for yourself."

"You, too."

He hung up, just like that. Pat stared at the receiver for a moment, then put it slowly back in the cradle. She brought her legs off the coffee table and curled them under her. Resting her head back on the seat cushion, she wept softly over what might have been. Any one of a hundred million people in America would love to switch places with her and lead her glamorous life. At this moment she was inclined to let them.

Oh, God, what avenging angel had come down to rob her of what she'd never deserved?

THE MAN GOT OFF THE ELEVATOR and walked directly to the apartment door marked 817. He rang the bell, its muffled tones playing the opening bars of "New York, New York."

The maid opened the door almost immediately. She was a young Hispanic woman, her faded jeans and baggy sweatshirt attesting to the notion that she wasn't expecting anyone.

"Good evening," he said, proffering a business card. "My name is Farley Masters, attorney at law, Houston, Texas. And you are...?"

"I'm Jesse," the woman said, her features hard. "Jesse Valez. Like I said on the phone, Mr. Masters, I can't help you. Miss Blackman is gone, and I don't know where she is."

"Yes, yes," the man said, smiling, his eyes nearly the same color as his pin-striped suit. "If I could just have a minute of your time, you'll understand what this is all about."

The woman hesitated, leaning against the edge of the door. "Miss Blackman doesn't like anybody in here when she—"

"Now, Jesse," he said, "this is something very special. Just a minute of your time."

"Oh...all right," the maid said, swinging the door open for his entry. "But don't tell Miss Blackman I let you in. I like this job, Mr. Masters."

"My lips are sealed." The man walked into the apartment, taking in its art deco style with a feeling of distaste. All flash, he thought. Blackman was a woman who simply squandered her gains to buy respectability for herself. Such an endeavor was always unsuccessful.

He sat on a batwing couch and laid his briefcase on the coffee table. "I am here on a matter of some delicacy," he said, watching the woman's face become somber. He opened the briefcase and pulled out an eight-by-ten of Jeff, then handed her the photograph.

The woman looked at the picture. "So?"

"I represent this young man," Blocker said. "He's Pat Blackman's son."

The woman began to laugh. "You come to the wrong place," she said, grinning. "Miss Blackman doesn't have a son. She's never been married."

"This is the twentieth century, Jesse," he responded. "One doesn't have to be married to have a child."

The maid frowned again, then looked at the picture intently. "I know what you mean," she said.

"The naked truth, if you'll pardon the expression, is that a Patty Blakowski had a child out of wedlock eighteen years ago and gave the baby up for adoption. Peter's family moved to Texas while he was still a baby, but as soon as he was old enough he began to search for his mother. It took two years, but he finally tracked down Miss Blackman, who had changed her name."

The woman was still holding the picture. "I guess I do see a family resemblance."

"Peter's a strange one," Blocker said. "He feels considerable anger toward Miss Blackman for never providing for his . . . how should I say it . . . support for all these years. He's really struggled, you see. His adopted family was killed in a car crash, and he lived in foster homes until he turned eighteen."

He pulled a stack of papers out of the briefcase and set them on the table. "Affidavits," he said, "attesting to all the things I've just told you. Anyway, now that he's found his mother, he feels she should help make things right for him. After all, she owes him at least that, don't you think?''

The woman put the picture down. "Oh, I don't know about that," she said quickly, realizing she wanted no part of this, yet knowing she was caught in the middle now.

"The problem, Jesse, is that Peter is so angry he wants to go to the newspapers with this and expose the history of neglect he's suffered all these years." Blocker shook his head. "It could get really sticky, if you know what I mean. What I want to do is get in touch with Miss Blackman myself and see if I can get this straightened out before Peter does something that everyone will be sorry for."

The woman shook her head. "I've got my orders."

"Let me put it another way, Jesse. Just suppose you don't help me and this finds its way to the papers, or maybe even national TV? What will Miss Blackman say if she finds out it was you who kept her from resolving this quietly?"

The woman thought about that for a moment. "I don't want to get mixed up in somebody's personal life, Mr. Masters. I'm just the household help, you know?"

"You know what kind of emergency this is, though, don't you?"

The woman took a breath, then nodded. She stood abruptly, having resolved some internal battle. "Wait right here," she said, and left the room.

Blocker stood and walked over to the sliding glass door that dominated the west wall of the apartment.

He opened the door and stepped out onto the patio, which looked out on late-night Fifth Avenue and East Sixty-eighth street. It provided a magnificent view of Central Park, just across Fifth. Prime New York real estate.

He walked back into the room, leaving the sliding door open. The woman was back in the room by the time he returned to the table. She was looking with narrowed eyes at the patio door.

"Incredible view," he said. "This apartment must cost a bundle."

Jesse Valez raised her eyebrows. "More than a bundle," she said, then held up the card index she carried. "I really don't know where Miss Blackman is, but her secretary, Miss Fisher, has the number. I was told to send any emergency calls over to her. You aren't on the emergency list, but like you say, this is a special emergency, right?"

"Right," Blocker replied. "And just between you and me, with this going to Miss Fisher, it takes you right off the hook, doesn't it?"

"Yeah." The woman sat on the sofa and flipped through the cards, stopping at the *F*'s. "Here it is. Miss Lydia Fisher, executive secretary."

"Excellent," Blocker said, moving back to sit next to her on the sofa. He reached into the upper pocket of the briefcase.

"You want me to call Miss Fisher for you?" the woman asked, standing.

"That won't be necessary," Blocker said, and the MAC-10 was in his hand.

"Wh-what are you...?"

Blocker smiled, putting a finger to his lips. "Please," he said. "Believe me, I'm not going to hurt you if you do exactly as I say."

"Oh, please, mister, please don't—"

"Shhh." He shook his head slightly, smiling. "I promise, no trouble—if you cooperate."

"Please, mister. Anything, just don't hurt me."

"Good. This won't be difficult, I promise. Now, Jesse, I want you to take off all your clothes."

The woman wrapped her arms protectively around her body. "What are you . . . you going to do?"

"Look," he said. "I promise. I just want to fix it so you won't go anywhere, you know?" He laughed, a deep basso. "I'm not going to rape you or anything. That's not my style. Now take your clothes off."

"No," she said.

"Oh, Jesse," he sighed, his hand shooting out to grab her arm. He took her by the hair and pulled hard, the barrel of the gun jammed tightly into her neck. "Do you see what happens the other way?" He pulled harder, her face contorting with pain, a scream choked in her throat.

She nodded vigorously, eyes wide. He stepped back, then politely said, "I'm sorry I had to do that. I really don't want any trouble. Now, please—your clothes."

She stripped perfunctorily. When she was naked, she wrapped her arms around her breasts, her lower lip trembling.

"Fold the clothes," Blocker demanded.

She did as she was told.

"Now," he said, "we're going to put them away."

He escorted her to her small apartment off the kitchen, watching intently as she placed the clothes in a chest of drawers.

"Let's put away the address file," he suggested, and dutifully marched back with her to the living room to retrieve the card index. He pulled out the important card, then they walked to an office just off the master bedroom and put the index on a walnut desk.

"Now what?" she asked, no longer covering herself, having decided that Blocker was as good as his word.

"The living room," he said. When they arrived, he asked, "How much do you weigh, Jesse?"

"A hundred and five pounds," she said, and he smiled wide, setting the Ingram on the coffee table.

He suddenly grabbed her and pulled her to him. She started to scream, but his fist found her open mouth, several teeth dissolving in a bloody froth. He grabbed her by the shoulder and left thigh, hoisting her above his head, and ran through the open sliding door to the patio.

Blocker hesitated for a second at the railing, then he used his great strength to propel her over the edge, angling her to fall away from the apartment so it would be difficult to ascertain which unit she'd come from.

She never screamed, never made a sound, as her body plummeted eight stories into the heavy evening traffic of Fifth Avenue.

Blocker didn't stay to watch her hit the pavement. He quietly closed the sliding door and returned to the coffee table to repack his briefcase. He straightened and looked around once, then left, locking the door behind him.

The ride down went quickly, and when he reached the lobby, the doorman was already on the street, joining the crowd to see what the commotion was. Blocker tore the page from the sign-in register, then walked out to merge with the pedestrian traffic.

5

Bolan encountered the first roadblock at the corner of Wexler and Canyon Road, just off the Sunset Strip. Two uniformed cops held him and Joan Meredith at the barricade while they checked their government IDs, first under the beam of a flashlight, then on their squad car radio.

Though it was nearly 2:00 a.m., the street beyond the barricade was alive with activity. Police cars, lab vans and TV news trucks and end-to-end reporters' cars filled the upgrade that was now cut off from all traffic. It was as if a whole new population had moved into the neighborhood and shoved the other residents out.

"It's a damned carnival," Joan said, her voice edgy as they watched the street, which was crowded with reporters who swarmed every human being emerging from behind the iron bars that were supposed to protect the estate from intruders. "They're just like vultures."

"Free country," Bolan replied, but didn't like it any better than she did. Events such as these always brought out the darker, ghoulish side of the human animal.

One of the cops returned to Bolan's rented Chevy, while the other hurried to move the barricade. The cop at the window handed back their IDs. "Just show your identification to the men at the gate," he said. "When they let you in, look for Sergeant Harrison. He's your liaison."

The cop stood back and waved them through; a long line of cars filled with curiosity seekers stretched out behind them. Bolan drove through, honking his horn to drive back the gnatlike reporters. He didn't much like the term "liaison." It smacked of a lockout to him, a siphoned information station where he would be given access to little more than the reporters got. It wasn't going to work with him. Not a bit.

"If things get sticky," Joan said, "let me handle it."

Bolan gave her a sidelong glance as he pulled up to the big iron gates and held up his ID for the cops to see. "What's that supposed to mean?" he asked. "What did Hal tell you?"

"This may need a delicate touch, that's all," the woman responded, fixing him with a neutral look.

"You don't think I'm capable of delicacy?" he asked as the police moved to open the gates.

"This is politics, Mack," Joan responded. "How we do things is just as important as what we do."

"You've been sent along to watchdog me, haven't you?" Bolan said, angry at Hal.

"It's not you against the world. We're representing the United States government."

Bolan pulled onto the grounds, police floodlights making the whole place look like a movie sound stage as blue suits searched the estate for clues. He parked near the large Southern-style house beside a line of black-and-whites, then turned in his seat to stare at the woman. She met his gaze head-on, never wavering.

"I can only do what I can do," he said.

"I'm surprised Brognola's letting you handle this one," she replied. "But you're in, and you are committed to an entirely different mode of behavior. Your credentials make you a personal representative of the President. Up here in the rarefied air, a lot depends on very little."

Bolan's jaw muscles tightened, but he heard the truth of her words. "Okay," he said. "You've scored a couple of times. I'm trading access for decorum, and it may be worth the trouble."

He started out of the car, but she stopped him with a hand on his arm. "And just for the record," she said, "Hal didn't send me here as a watchdog. He asked me to come with you and render whatever assistance I could, period."

He nodded.

They got out of the car, the woman lugging a case that contained a small computer she refused to let anyone touch.

As they started around the loose gravel drive toward the big front doors, a man in a dark suit and thick glasses came out and approached them. He met them ten feet from the entrance, looking extremely tired.

"You must be the government people, Belasko and Meredith," he said, extending a hand to Bolan, then Meredith. "My name's Sergeant Mike Harrison. They told me to explain things to you."

"I'd like to see the house," Bolan said.

Harrison grimaced. "Why don't we talk out here? There's enough confusion inside as it is. Now, what is it that the President could want to know about all this? Was he friends with the actor?"

"I don't know," Bolan said coldly. "I'm interested in the terrorist angle in all this."

"The what?" Harrison asked, his tired face crinkling into a smile. "There are no terrorists here, Mr. Belasko."

"What makes you so sure?" the woman asked.

The man shrugged. "Well, I mean, this is homicide...movie murder. What in heaven's name would bring terrorists up into the Hollywood Hills to come after *this* particular man?"

"What about the tape?" Bolan asked.

"Crazy smoke screen," Harrison said, reaching into his shirt pocket for a cigarette. "You want to hear my theory? It's some actors gone schizo who played out this big scene for the cameras...you know, like they were in a real movie or something. This town is full of nuts."

He stuck the cigarette in his mouth and pulled out a disposable lighter.

"I prefer that you don't smoke," Joan said as Harrison was about to fire the tobacco. He hesitated for a second, then put out the flame.

"Sure, Miss Meredith," he said. "Anything to accommodate the government." He stuck the cigarette in a pocket of his rumpled jacket.

"What kind of leads do you have?" Bolan asked as he watched a K-9 unit amble past, the big dogs whimpering and sniffing the Bermuda grass.

The policeman glanced away. "Well, not much. There's no sign of entry onto the property or into the house, though a back door was wired shut. They cut the phone lines and some of the power lines."

"*Some* of the power lines?" Joan asked.

"Yeah," Harrison said, pushing his glasses higher up on his nose. "They, ah, cut the alarm systems only, and they also took out the streetlight on Wexler."

"They also killed the caretaker, didn't they?" Bolan asked.

"Yeah," the man said quietly.

Bolan pushed on. "What about the tapes? Anything on how they made the duplicates?"

Harrison was looking uncomfortable. "Think so. There's a guy who runs a duping service a little farther down Sunset who works out of his house and specializes in all-night service."

"He did the duplication?"

"Well, I don't know. He was . . . killed last night, too. Shot up with automatic fire just like these folks."

"Pretty smart crazy men," Bolan said. "They murdered seven people, got in and out without a trace and ran the whole thing like a military operation."

Several cops walked past, talking and drinking coffee out of paper cups. Large flashlights hung on their belts. Harrison looked at them for a moment, then motioned for Bolan and Meredith to follow him out of their range of hearing. They moved over into the crooked maze of parked police cars, finding themselves a space in the center of the lot.

"Look," Harrison said softly, "I'll be completely honest. This thing has got us stymied from the word go." His hand moved to his pocket again, and he stopped himself, looking at Joan. "Do you *really* mind?"

"Go ahead. I just wanted to get your attention before."

He raised an eyebrow, then lit a cigarette, smoke spilling from his mouth as he talked. "We're just cops, you know? What are we supposed to do when some creeps start talking international politics? They sounded like Americans to me! Hell, I *know* it's too slick for a crazy man, but what am I supposed to do, go arrest Khaddafi? Our hands are tied and retied. We've got no choice but to pursue this as a regular homicide, maybe a serial thing. Anything else is out of our jurisdiction."

"Who's jurisdiction is it, then?" Bolan asked. "Ours?"

"No way, José," the man replied, taking a deep drag from his cigarette. "This doesn't fit FBI territory yet, and the last thing Captain Merkle is going to do is let somebody else come in to muck up *our* investigation."

"Captain Merkle," Meredith said. "Is that Charlie Merkle?"

"Yeah. You know him?"

The woman smiled. "Yeah. He was Lieutenant Merkle then, but he gave me a break back when nobody wanted women on the force."

Harrison looked hard at her, his lips slowly stretching into a grin. "Good God, I thought I recognized you. You're the woman who iced those three hoods in the warehouse that night your backup deserted you. Got a commendation from the governor, didn't you?"

She looked at the ground. "They were playing up women's roles then," she said.

"Well, let me play it totally straight with an excop," Harrison said. "Go back to Washington. Tell them we've got it under control. There's nothing you can do out here, anyway, and the captain sure as hell isn't going to let you two muck around in the middle of this. This damned thing's sensational enough without the government sticking its nose in. If anyone began believing this terrorist crap, it could start a bona fide panic."

"It's not crap," Bolan said.

Harrison stared at him for several long seconds. "What?"

"I believe that this operation was carried out by professional terrorists, and that it's just the first of many attacks. Now, Sergeant, we'd like to go inside the house."

"Screw that," Harrison said, throwing his cigarette on the ground and stomping on it.

Bolan started moving through the cars. "I'm going in."

"I'll be goddamned," the other man responded, and started after him.

"Wait," Meredith said, "we'll make a deal with you."

"What kind of deal?" Harrison asked.

"If you let us in without any hassles, Mr. Belasko won't go outside those gates and tell the news media his theory on the murders."

"That sounds like a threat to me," Harrison replied, then looked at Bolan. "Just who the hell are you?"

The Executioner just stared at him. "Is it a go?"

Harrison took off his glasses and rubbed his eyes with his fingertips. "If I were you, I wouldn't want any part of this," he said after a moment. "I've been on the force for nearly twenty years. But when I walked in there this morning and saw those bodies…I broke down and cried like a baby. Didn't think I could do that anymore. You want it, you got it. Come on."

He led them back to the house and past the yellow police crime-scene tape wrapped around the entryway. Inside was a madhouse of technicians, dusting the entire house for fingerprints. It appeared that no expense was being spared on this thing, but to Bolan it was all useless. They'd find nothing.

As they walked through a formal living room, Harrison pointed to a fireplace. "They burned their coveralls in here," he said. "There were some small pieces left, but not enough to do any good. We found a section of collar, but the tag had been cut off."

They moved into the den. Bolan thought about the coveralls and how only serious premeditation and experience would prepare someone for the splattering of blood from close-range killing.

He recognized the killing room immediately from the tape, enough so that it sent a chill down his back. The exploded television sat in ruins on the beige carpet. A man in a lab coat moved around under the police floodlights, videotaping the scene.

A man in a suit sat on the couch where the victims had sat. He was leaning forward, his head in his hands. On the floor, where they had fallen, lay the silhouettes of the dead, marked out in tape, huge areas of blood still staining the carpet.

"Captain Merkle," Harrison said, and the man looked up slowly. "These are the government people. They wanted to see the scene."

"Just stay out of my way," Merkle growled, then his eyes lighted on Meredith. "Joanie? Is that you?"

As she moved toward him, the man stood to embrace her. "How are you, Charlie?" she said. "I see you're moving up in the world."

"You, too," he replied, then sat back down. "Hell of a place for a reunion."

"This is my partner, Mike Belasko," she said. Merkle reaching out to shake hands. To Bolan, the man looked even more tired than Harrison, the pressure affecting him directly.

"Have you got anything?" Bolan asked.

Merkle let his eyes drift to Harrison.

"I told them everything," the man admitted.

"That's it then," Merkle said. "No government business, just murder, and a hell of a public relations job."

"Have the phones been fixed?" Joan asked.

Merkle nodded. "Try the kitchen. Harrison will show you where it is."

"Thanks."

"Tell me about Seales," Bolan said.

"Tell me about Seales," Bolan said.

Merkle stared at him for a moment, then apparently decided it was easier to go along. "Successful filmmaker. Hollywood god. His first feature film came in in '73, one of those teenage coming-of-age things that grossed about a hundred mil. He made a picture every couple of years or so—space wars, adventure—provided a lot of jobs in this town. Then he went respectable a couple of years back and made an "important" picture and won some awards. You know, that sort of success builds its own kind of lunatic fringe following, like the guy who shot John Lennon."

"How about foreign travel or financing for his pictures?" Bolan asked.

"Forget that line of thinking," the man snapped. "Tell your friends in the White House that we have the situation under control."

"But you don't," Bolan said. "You need to be working on Seales's ties to Libya. What are you doing in that area?"

Merkle was on his feet again. He was as large as Bolan and a little beefier. "The only reason you're standing in here right now, mister, is because of old times and Joan Meredith. Don't push your good fortune. I don't care about your fancy authorization or credentials."

"Neither do I," Bolan said. "All I care about is stopping this man before he reaches the next victim on his list. Why don't you climb down off your high horse and start staring reality in the face."

"That's it!" Merkle bellowed. "Get out. You've had your cooperation."

Bolan stood his ground. "I'm just asking you to sift through his life, that's all. Find out what's there. This was a professional job, and you know it. There must be a motivation."

"Out of here and off the property," Merkle ordered, veins bulging on his forehead. "Or I'll throw you out myself."

Bolan took a step toward him.

"No wonder the world's in such a sorry state," Meredith said. She stood in the kitchen doorway scowling. "Leave you alone for five minutes and you're at each other's throat."

"Take him out of here, Joanie," Merkle said. "Anything else you want, go through Harrison on the phone. Don't try and come out here anymore."

"I can't believe..." Bolan began, but the woman took him by the arm, and pulled him in the direction of the front door.

The big man let her propel him along, his gut churning. It was always the same, a near impossibility to change a tight mind-set. The sheer waste of time and manpower in such a huge operation drove him nearly to distraction. All this time wasted spinning wheels while the terrorist was out as free as the breeze, planning the next hit.

Meredith got him out the door and started him across the lawn. "You're in good form, I see. You've managed to alienate every cop you've met so far."

"Stow it, would you? Where were you when I needed you back with your old chum?"

"Getting information," she replied, "real information."

"What have you got?"

"In the car," she said.

They moved to the car and climbed in, the woman leaving her door partly open so the dome light would stay on. She opened her case and produced several sheets of printout paper and handed them to him.

"While we were playing footsie with Charlie," she said, "it struck me that we have access to more channels than he does when it comes to finding out about someone's past."

Bolan looked over the pages. "These are income tax returns," he said.

She smiled broadly. "Yep. I hooked my modem up to their phone and used my authorization to get into the authorization file and came up with the passwords in the IRS computers where they keep the records. I had to go back a way, but I found that at one time John Seales was a cameraman working overseas assignments for CBS."

Bolan stared at the information. Seales had apparently stayed out of the country for a continuous period of eighteen months in the late sixties and had requested, as per the law, that income taxes paid for that period be returned to him. The request was filed in 1969, the same year that Khaddafi took power in Libya.

"It's not much," Meredith said.

"But it's a start," Bolan replied. "Now..."

"Now we get to find some rooms and get a night's sleep," the woman said. "This can wait till the morning."

Bolan started the car and put it into gear, wondering if the man with the Freon eyes was sleeping right now.

BLOCKER STOOD at the bathroom sink, washing the blood off his hands. "I have simply *got* to tell you, Miss Fisher, that you have put up one *hell* of a fight." He put a hand to his lips. "Oops. Pardon my French."

He turned to the woman, the red of her blood on the tiles standing out in stark contrast to the bright, garish white of the rest of the room.

He finished rinsing his hands and wiped them on the white towel on the rack. Then he sat on the edge of the tub and looked at her. She was one tough old woman, gray hair, wrinkled lips and all, and she could swing a baseball bat with the best of them. She lay in the tub, an arm broken and twisted under her at a grotesque angle. The left side of her face was puffing badly, the skin already beginning to discolor. Blood flowed freely from several cuts, pooling around her in the tub, staining her flower-printed housedress a rust color.

"I've never been to Long Island before," he said. "It's really not bad, cosmopolitan and suburban, too. I think I've always wanted to live in a place like this. You have a nice house. I'll bet it was really cozy when you lived here with your husband, God rest his soul."

The woman tried to move, groaning loudly.

Blocker clucked loudly. "Don't try, ma'am," he soothed. "You'll just hurt yourself more. Just take it easy now. It's all over."

Loreen came to the door, an ice bag pressed to her temple.

"How ya feeling, honey?" he asked in a Southern accent.

"Shove it, Farley," she snarled. "That old bitch nearly took my head off. I almost blacked out back there, and my head's killing me."

The man showed empty palms. "Rough," he said. "How are the kids doing?"

"They haven't found anything yet."

"Okay. Well, I think that me and Miss Fisher have reached an agreement of sorts, and we're going to have another little talk. Go help the kids."

Loreen glared at the old woman, her eyes deep with hatred. "When you do it—"

"Now, Loreen, nobody's going to do anything. Go on."

She turned and left, Blocker leaning down close to the old woman's face. She still showed no fear, and he was glad to see such spunk. "I don't think Loreen likes you very much," he said. "I don't think you'd like me to turn you over to her, would you?"

"Go to hell," the woman rasped.

Blocker smiled broadly again. "I declare, you are one tough old bird. But we don't have all night. Now, you've given us the phone number, but not the location. No employer can be worth this kind of pain, Miss Fisher. Just tell us where she is."

"She wouldn't say," the woman said, her voice weak. "Sh-she didn't want anyone to know. That was the point."

"But you're closer to her than anyone. Surely she would tell you."

"I d-don't know . . . where she . . . is."

"Tell you what," Blocker said. "Let's wash some of that blood off you. You look a fright."

He leaned across her and turned on the hot water, then pulled the shower knob. "I'll just bet you keep your water tank real hot to get those dishes good and clean, don't you?"

The woman's eyes widened as the spray played across her body. She tried to rise again, but Blocker pushed her down. "It's going to heat up pretty quick," he said. "I think you'd better tell me."

Within seconds, the room began to fill with steam, and the man stuffed a washcloth in Miss Fisher's mouth. He turned and walked out of the bathroom into the shambles of the rest of the house.

The others were concentrating their efforts on the small bedroom the woman had converted to an office. They were dismantling the place piece by piece.

"I guess she was telling the truth," he said, picking up the piece of paper that contained the Blackman woman's number.

Loreen looked at him expectedly. The whole side of her face had turned a livid red-purple. "Did you . . . ?"

"Naw," he said. "I saved her for you. Tomorrow morning we're going to have to get a long wig to cover that side of your face."

Loreen left the room as the two teenagers gleefully tore the couch to pieces with butcher knives from the kitchen, pulling out handfuls of foam rubber padding.

Blocker picked up a telephone directory he found amid the rubble on the floor and opened it to the front section containing the area codes. He spent a minute going through the book, stopping when he reached the 505 code.

"Hurry it up, Loreen!" he called. "We're going to New Mexico!"

6

Bolan sat behind the wheel of the Chevy, watching the spray-painted gang turf of West L.A. slide past the windows and listening to the man from the network affiliate who sat in the back seat.

"You can't really expect anything," the man, Riley, said. "We keep some things in the vaults, but we can't keep everything. Twenty years is a long time."

"The government appreciates your cooperation on this matter," Joan said sweetly from beside Bolan. "It isn't always that the news media and the White House get to work together."

"Yeah," Riley replied. "Maybe we'll set a precedent or something."

They talked on and on, Bolan only partially listening. He had sat up most of the night, preparing himself for the combat that would eventually come. As soon as he'd found a trail with a scent to it, he had felt the change within himself. His adversary was more than just a shadow now. He was flesh and blood, and though he didn't know it yet, he would be going head-to-head with the Executioner.

Bolan had spent the night cleaning his guns, a ritual that always seemed to relax him and prepare him mentally for what was to come. Freon bothered Bolan. Like a bizarre alter ego, this savage for hire trod the same ground Bolan trod, frequented the same haunts, did business with the same sort of people. They were opposite sides of the same coin, and it sickened Bolan to know that comparisons were unavoidable. He had to stop this thing lest he lose himself to its darkness. And that kind of feeling he could never explain to anyone, nor hope that it could be understood. All he knew was that getting Freon was absolutely essential.

"...huge funerals," Riley was saying. "This town hasn't seen anything like it since Marilyn Monroe OD'd. They turned out in droves for that one. Elvis had a big funeral, too. This isn't bad for us locally because we're getting a lot of the national exposure on the coverage for our in-town news teams. And that will help some résumés...including mine."

"Why is this warehouse so far from the station?" Meredith asked.

"Hell, we got warehouses all over the damned country," Riley replied. "Lots of film and tape gets turned out over the years. If you're going to keep any of it, you start running into storage problems. That's why so much film and tape is missing. It's just too damned expensive to keep storing it. Turn left here."

The man pointed, and Bolan turned down a narrow alleyway between a grocery store and a nude wrestling parlor. "Stop here."

Riley directed them to a doorway set into the same building as the grocery. Bolan pulled up beside it, blocking the whole alley. They climbed out and were assaulted by the sickly-sweet smell of rotting garbage. Riley opened the door with a large key.

It was cold and dry in there, like a refrigerator. Riley flipped a light switch, and rows of long tubes stuttered to life and lit the place with an unreal neon glow.

They were standing in a huge open room filled with free-standing metal shelves all crammed with film cans. There might have been a hundred thousand different reels of film there.

"Here you are," Riley announced, his middle-aged face smiling dryly. "Good luck."

Meredith, already sorry she had dressed so casually, was hugging herself against the cold of the room. "Is there any order to all this?" she asked.

"Not that I know of," came the reply.

Bolan felt his stomach tighten. They could lose precious hours here, looking for a piece of film that might not exist. They had ascertained from CBS records in New York that cameraman John Seales had covered uprisings in Rhodesia and the Middle East through 1968 and 1969, and they had a record of a story being filed from Tripoli toward the end of 1969. Right after the story, Seales had come back to the States and resigned his post with CBS to venture into independent filmmaking. If that piece of film existed at all, it was reasoned to be in the Los Angeles storage facility off El Secundo Boulevard. But there were no guarantees, none at all. The rules for saving film weren't hard and fast. So there was nothing to do but dig into the business at hand.

Two hours passed, and the three of them were chilled to the bone. Bolan had spent the first hour walking through the building, looking for rhyme or reason to the storage. The cans were all marked, and even some of the shelves had years written on them, but it didn't seem to affect what was stored in that place. Finally realizing the futility of searching for logic, he simply picked a shelf and started going through the cans, reading what was written on the tape that banded them closed.

Bolan was sifting through a whole stack of Walter Cronkite reports from Korea when he heard Joan scream.

"I've got it! We've hit pay dirt!"

Bolan dropped the cans he held and charged to where she stood. The tape read: Libya October 1969. Feature—5:30.

Riley was at his shoulder. "Think you've got something there," he said. "Want to roll it through the projector?"

"You've got one here?" Bolan asked.

The man nodded. "Got a little screening room off to the side. Come on."

They found the cleared-out section. Riley had already pulled down a large white screen from the ceiling and set up three folding chairs. The projector sat behind a concrete wall, its lens poking through a cutout in the concrete.

Riley took the film can and disappeared behind the partition, a few minutes later calling out, "Hit that light switch on the wall near you."

Bolan hit the lights and went back to sit next to Joan.

A picture wound out on the screen. The film had faded somewhat, the color washed out, but it was still watchable. It showed a panoramic shot of a Middle Eastern seaport, dirty, rusted freighters stacked in against the blue-green of the Mediterranean. He recognized the port immediately as Tripoli, Libya, remarkably unchanged in the ensuing years. It was late afternoon in the film, the pictures obviously being taken from the balcony of a hotel. A voice began to narrate.

"Tripoli," the voice said. "The gateway to Africa, to its people, to its vast resources. Here is the trade capital of the United Federal Kingdom of Libya where the Phoenicians first linked the country to the outside world by settling in this city in 800 B.C."

Bolan sat up straight, listening intently to the voice coming through the speaker mounted on the ceiling. It sounded incredibly familiar, but he couldn't quite place it.

The speaker continued. "Libya is a land of contrasts, of goat carts and date palms on the one hand and hard-nosed industrialism on the other. A pastoral nation that is ninety percent unfarmable desert. A poor nation that nevertheless has an annual budget of two hundred and fifty million for fewer than two million people. Why?"

"The reason is this." The camera switched to a close-up of a small jar being held in a man's hand. Black liquid filled the jar. "Oil," the voice continued. "Modern man's equivalent of the Midas touch. Libya is soaked in it, filthy with it, and like Midas's golden touch, it could prove just as dangerous."

The camera pulled back to reveal a young man dressed in khaki. His hair was fashionably long on the temples, the sideburns meeting his jawline.

The man was younger, but there was no mistaking the lanky frame, baby face and melodious voice.

"Jake Torrance," Joan breathed, awed. And it was. Senator Jake Torrance, presidential candidate. Bolan wished he could see on the other side of the camera to see if John Seales was manning it. The stakes were suddenly getting higher. The man kept talking.

"Ninety-nine percent of Libya's now-burgeoning economy is dominated by an oil industry that simply continues to grow and prosper beyond all reason. A devout Muslim country that has as its eastern neighbor the United Arab Republic, Libya, thanks to the oil boom, is suddenly finding itself in a new leadership position among Arab nations. And it is also drawing the attention of others."

The scene switched to a shot taken through the window of a restaurant, looking across the street to a hotel where a huge limo was pulling up. Torrance's voice narrated over the action. "Those men getting out of the car are Russian negotiators come to pay their respects. They are visiting this man...."

The camera zoomed in for a close-up of a man in uniform shaking hands with the Russian delegation.

"Moammar Khaddafi is the new ruler of this prosperous nation, replacing King Idris #I, who had ruled since independence in 1951. Idris was a moderate, a friend of the United States, who had always tried to balance what he felt to be the extremes of Arab politics with an even hand. Many felt that Idris had become old and tired. Khaddafi has none of these problems.''

"The colonel, as he likes to call himself, is a modern Arab in every sense of the word. He is committed to expansion, committed to Arab unity in the export of oil, committed to the expulsion of Israel from the Middle East at any cost. The U.S., unwilling to lose a necessary friend in North Africa has been courting the colonel with bouquets of fighter planes, F-4 Phantoms that the Libyan leader wants desperately. Khaddafi has been careful to accept the hand of friendship from President Nixon, even going as far as making promises of neutrality in Arab politics in exchange for the planes. But does he mean it?''

The scene switched again, this time to a hiding place behind a stand of rocks that looked out over the Libyan desert. The camera was shaky, obviously handheld, as it peeked around the rocks to show a view of an installation going up in the desert, a series of tracks and bunkers, with Khaddafi and the Russian delegation inspecting it.

Bolan recognized the type of construction immediately. "Missile base," he whispered.

"This is an ICBM installation under construction," Torrance said, "the tracks for the movement of the bombs themselves, the bunkers for the soldiers who man them. The targets are Israel and the United States. Our cameraman, John Seales, got these shots at great personal risk.''

The scene switched back to Torrance, who stood on the same balcony overlooking the city. "So while Colonel Khaddafi is welcoming Nixon with his right hand, his left is ready to push the button that will annihilate us. We can sit here on our balcony and watch Russian ambassadors, engineers and technicians come and go all day and night. It is a frightening and sobering sight, for we feel we are watching the restructuring of the Middle East because of American need for oil and our friendship with Israel. One more ace has been stacked in the deck against American interests in this part of the world. Is Moammar Khaddafi likely to become a friend of the United States?''

The scene changed to the previous one outside the hotel, showing Khaddafi embracing the Russians, one by one.

''Our investigations point to a loud and resounding no. This is Jake Torrance, CBS news, Tripoli.''

The film ended, a hastily scrawled credit list written on a small chalkboard tagged onto the end. It contained three names: Jake Torrance, John Seales and someone named Patty Blakowski, who was listed as researcher and script consultant. Then the film ran through, bright white replacing the images on the screen.

The room went dark again.

''Get the lights!'' Riley called.

Bolan felt numb as he stood to move to the wall. When he came back, Meredith was staring at him. ''I don't think I ever really believed you,'' she said quietly, shaking her head. ''But this is...is a solid connection.''

Bolan frowned. ''There's got to be more, though. A piece is still missing. How could Khaddafi let them film there? How could he let them get those shots?''

"Arrogance, maybe?" the woman suggested. "Holy hell. What more do you want? You've got the link you were looking for."

Bolan nodded, not sure why he felt so uneasy. Riley came out from behind the partition, the film can in his hands.

"Wow!" he said. "This is some hot stuff."

"We've got to get to a telephone," Bolan told Meredith. "We've got to get Torrance locked in."

"I remember this now," Riley said. "I was pretty new with the network then, but this was sensational. It even kicked Vietnam off the air for a while. I believe that on the strength of this we withdrew our offer of planes and weapons to the Libyans."

"There's your last connection," Joan said. "Khaddafi has held a grudge ever since they dumped on him."

Bolan frowned. It still didn't feel right. But that was a background concern. He felt he had the hit list now, and the trick was going to be stopping Freon before he got to the next name on the tear sheet.

"You know anything about this woman, Blakowski?" he asked Riley.

"You bet I do," he said. "We always remember the ones who get famous. After she got back from overseas, she changed her name to Blackman and started that magazine...what the heck's the name of it? *We*? *Us*?

"*You*!" Joan said loudly. "This is the same woman who publishes *You* Magazine?"

"Yep," he said, hugging the film can to his chest. "They all got famous. And now I'm going to get famous, because after twenty years in the business, I finally got a scoop!''

"Not yet," Bolan said, snatching the film from him. "This goes to Washington first. Maybe they can do some more research on it."

"Hey, that's private property," Riley protested. "You can't take that."

"It's a national security matter," Joan Meredith said, her tone finally matching Bolan's feelings. "Sorry."

BLOCKER STOOD at the grubby motel window and stared at the huge neon boot that served as the background for its logo: The Boots and Saddles Motor Inn. After taking a plane to Phoenix, Arizona, they had rented a car and driven to the New Mexico state line. It was 11:00 a.m., and they had the entire state, from midpoint, at their disposal.

Even though they had spelled one another with the driving through the early morning, Blocker was tired and knew he'd have to get a little more sleep before psyching up for the next part of the mission. After driving through the vast unsettled stretches of the American Southwest, he had begun to realize just how massive the country, and his job, really were. It was desert country, hard and uncompromising, and he'd need to toughen up even more to see the mission through. But he was smart, smarter than those who would come to look for him. And he had something that would stand him in good stead in this vast land—he was anonymous.

He drew the curtain, shutting out the broiling early-afternoon sun. The room was small, barely large enough for the two double beds that filled it. They had put the chain lock on the door and braced it with a board. Their belongings, ordnance and videocamera lay scattered around the room, the kids dropping them anywhere so they could get in front of the television to see if they had become famous.

He heard the shower stop, and Loreen appeared seconds later, dripping water, as she dried herself with a large white towel.

"I told you not to run around in front of the boy naked, Loreen," he growled.

"Go to hell, Blocker," she said, dropping the towel on the floor and standing in front of a full-length mirror to examine the discoloration on her face.

"And I told you not to call me that name," he said, moving to where she stood.

"Hey, look," Mary Ann called from where she sat on the edge of the bed. "We're on television!"

Blocker turned and saw Jeff pretending to look at the television, while his eyes continually flicked in Loreen's direction. Complications on a mission like this could be fatal. Loreen should be professional enough to appreciate that.

The man walked up behind her as she studied her face. He put his hands on her shoulder blades and began a massage. Her eyes stared at him as he towered above her in the mirror image.

"You know what I can do with ten million dollars?" he asked.

She just stared at him, not answering.

"If I wanted, I could live on it for the rest of my life," he said, answering his own question. He began to apply subtle pressure to her shoulders. "If I wanted, I could buy myself an island somewhere and live on it. I could buy a bunch of aircraft. I could buy thousands of women that men would kill for. I could have the best of everything for as long as I lived." He squeezed harder, the pressure making her wince.

"Bloc—" she started, but fell silent.

"Do you know how much your miserable life stacks up against all that, Loreen?" He hit a pressure point and dug in, the pain racking her. Her knees weakened, nearly taking her to the floor.

He bent with her. "I'd cut you up in little pieces and flush you down the toilet right now if I thought you'd do something to jeopardize this deal, and don't think I wouldn't."

Her eyes were wide, frightened. "Bl—Farley... don't."

He pulled her to her feet, twisting her arms painfully behind her. "Jeff," he called. "Get your butt over here."

"Yes, sir."

The boy moved to them, his eyes wide as he looked at the woman.

"Put your hands all over her, boy," he ordered, pulling Loreen back, bending her over like a taut bow.

"Pardon?"

"You want to," Blocker said. "Put your hands all over her, go ahead."

"No," Loreen said.

The boy hesitated, but Blocker nodded, and he did what he was told with enthusiasm.

Loreen twisted in his grasp, eyes shut tightly, face strained.

"Do you like it?" Blocker asked her. "Is this what you wanted?"

"Farley...please."

"That's enough, Jeff," the man commanded, and the boy backed away reluctantly.

He threw the woman to the floor. "You start taking this seriously, or we'll end it right here," he said. "And get some damned clothes on, bitch. Now."

As Loreen scrabbled to her feet, Blocker turned and pointed a finger at Jeff. "And if you ever touch her again, I'll cut your hands off, understand?"

"Yes, sir," the boy said, moving back sheepishly to the bed.

"Come and watch," Mary Ann said, waving an arm to them. "They're showing our movie."

The man walked over to the TV and watched as the video they'd made was replayed on the news show in skip jumps, most of the more graphic violence cut out. The kids loved it, giggling and poking each other when they spoke or performed any action. Mary Ann got especially worked up, her body vibrating all over the bed as she relived every moment.

As the clip was winding down, Loreen, in a large terry-cloth robe, went over to the bed and sat next to Blocker, taking his hand in hers.

"I'm sorry, Farley," she said contritely.

"It's okay," he said, tousling her hair. "We just needed to get that out of the way. Now, I've got a call to make. Turn down the tube," he said, picking up the telephone receiver. The sound went down, and he dialed the number he had gotten from the Fisher woman, putting the long-distance call on Farley's credit card.

He'd still have to find out exactly where Blackman was. New Mexico was a large state, and it only had one area code. The phone rang several times before a woman with a monotone voice answered. He asked for Miss Blackman and was told to wait.

After several minutes, a tentative voice came on the line. "Hello," she said in a small voice.

"Is this Pat Blackman?" he asked officiously.

"Y-yes it is," she returned, her voice shaky.

"This is Daniel Turner with the Federal Bureau of Investigation."

"Oh, my God," she said.

"You're in a great deal of trouble, Miss Blackman," he said. "You should have come to us after the first murder instead of running away. You've endangered many lives by your thoughtless actions."

"I was frightened, I—"

"Look, Miss Blackman. We know the whole story, and we know why you ran, so you can stop playing games right now."

"Please, I'm sorry, I—"

"Miss Blackman. This isn't the time. Those killers are still on the loose, and we're really very busy on the investigation. We're going to need to send someone out there to protect you."

"How did you...find me?"

"A Miss Lydia...Fisher, your secretary, gave us the number after we contacted her concerning this matter."

"I mean, how did you find where I was?"

"Once we had the number, we simply traced you down through the telephone company." He opened the road atlas to New Mexico and picked a town at random. "It seems to me that the closest town to you is...Socorro."

"You mean the closest large city?" she replied. "There are several small towns a lot closer to us than that."

"Have they got a police department, though?"

"Trechado does," she replied. "I saw one when we passed through. We're only about ten miles west of there off Highway 36."

Blocker smiled, writing down the information. "Trechado it is, then," he said. "What's your status right now. Are you safe?"

"I have ten armed bodyguards here with me."

"Good," he said. "I'm not nearby yet. It's going to take me a few hours to finish up what I'm doing and get down there. I'll round up the Trechado sheriff, and we'll come out your way in the squad car later this evening to escort you back to town so we can question you and keep an eye on you."

"Can I...bring my bodyguards?"

"You can bring a whole convoy of them if you want," he said. "It's your payroll, not mine."

"Am I...in trouble?"

"Some," he answered. "Cooperation at this point will mean a lot. Look, miss. We're just trying to catch a murderer and protect you as best we can. Let's just keep that in mind.''

"My secretary—" the woman began.

"Your secretary's in protective custody right now like you should be. Your best bet at this point is to keep a low profile. Make no outside calls. If you have trouble or need anything, call the sheriff's department in Trechado. They'll take any messages for me. And don't let any vehicles near your place except the squad car, all right?''

"Yes, sir."

"Good. Stay alert. Stay alive. We'll see you tonight.''

"Yes, sir." She hung up.

Blocker immediately called New Mexico information to get the number of the Trechado police. He wrote down the number, then cradled the receiver on his shoulder.

"Turn off that television," he said, "and get some sleep." He looked at his watch. "At 1300 we move out. We've got a police car to steal and business to take care of.''

He dialed the number of the police station, enjoying the respect that Daniel Turner, FBI, seemed to engender.

"I DON'T WANT TO TALK to you, Trevans," Bolan said angrily into the phone. "I want the senator on the line, right now.''

"The senator's busy," the Secret Serviceman replied. "Or have you forgotten that he's running for president.''

"Just get him."

"I can't," the man answered. "He's on television at the moment. What do you want."

"You've been briefed?"

"Yeah, I've been briefed, and I can handle Torrance's protection just fine without your interference."

"That's what you said back in Virginia," Bolan said.

"Get off my back, you son of a bitch," Trevans replied. "I didn't need you then, and I don't need you now."

"I don't think you understand just how seri—"

"Screw off!" Trevans yelled, and slammed the receiver down.

Bolan sat back on the motel bed and dropped the receiver back in the cradle. With Trevans in charge of Jake Torrance's protection, they could be in a world of hurt despite the extra men Justice had assigned to the duty. He had wanted to talk with Torrance, to ask him just what the story was, but for the moment that would have to wait.

He stood, stretching, and could hear Joan Meredith's voice on the phone in the connecting room. He walked to the door that separated the rooms and knocked lightly before pushing through. The woman sat on the king-size bed talking animatedly on the phone, her computer set up on a coffee table nearby.

"Nothing?" she said. "Who have they questioned? You're kidding!"

Bolan moved into her line of vision, shrugging a question.

Her eyes widened, and she shook her head. "I can't believe that nobody has anything."

Bolan looked at his watch. It was 11:00 a.m. The killers had been loose and on the run for close to thirty-six hours. They could be anywhere in the country.

"All right," Joan said. "Try to keep us posted."

She hung up the phone and ran a hand through her short hair. "Pat Blackman is on the run," she said, "and apparently nobody knows where she is. Her executive secretary supposedly had her phone number in case of emergency...."

"And?"

"And they found her dead this morning... mangled. She'd been savagely beaten and scalded. She finally died from blood loss after being slashed over a hundred times with a razor blade. Her house had been turned upside down."

"Damn!"

She put up a hand. "And there's more. Blackman's maid was also killed, or so it appears. She either jumped or was thrown from the balcony of Blackman's eighth-floor apartment. It took all night for them to make positive ID because she was naked, no identification at all."

Bolan drove a fist into an open palm. "Eight dead now that we know about. There were no leads?"

The woman shook her head. "The police and our people have questioned everyone who had anything to do with her, from her employees to her dry cleaners. One minute she was the center of the universe, the next she was a black hole."

"She's on the run," Bolan said. "She took off after hearing about Seales. I know there's more to this than just the film." He walked over to stare at Meredith's computer, idly playing his fingers on the keyboard.

"We need to catch a plane for Washington," she said, standing. "They want us back with the newsreel film and debriefing."

"No," Bolan said.

"What?"

"I'm not going back to Washington," he said.

"But we have to."

He turned to her. "No, *you* have to. I don't have to do anything."

"Mack—"

"Listen to me, Joan." He went over to the bed and sat down beside her. "Freon's out there on the loose. He's tracking that woman right now. He'll eventually find her and kill her and anybody else who's with her. Then he'll go after Jake Torrance, kill him and anybody around him. He'll kill and keep on killing until I stop him."

"Until you stop him," she said, narrowing her eyes.

"You don't get it, do you? In Washington and in the police departments they'll follow regulations, get wound up in red tape, try and figure out the right thing to do, the right office to call, the proper authorizations to take out. And meanwhile, Freon will be killing and feeling stronger with every kill. You know how they catch serial killers? By accident. They got Son of Sam on a parking violation, the Boston Strangler the same way. Those people were nuts and made stupid mistakes, and even at that they got away with murder after murder. Well, Freon isn't nuts. He's as cold as ice, and he doesn't make stupid mistakes. He's a machine, a killing machine.''

"You act like you know him," she said quietly.

"I know *exactly* how his mind's working as he picks his killzones and covers his trail. That's why I can't go back. I'm on his wavelength right now. I've got to keep on the move, to keep dogging him. He's got a jump now, but I think I can narrow the gap. The only way to catch this guy is to think like he thinks and keep on dogging him, forcing him to get sloppy, to make that fatal mistake. If I get caught up in the red tape, it'll be worse than handcuffs and leg irons." He walked to the computer again. "No, Joan. I'm not going back to Washington."

She looked at him. "I saw you tightening up, wondered what was happening. You've been down some roads, haven't you?"

"I'm a goddamned map, lady. And it's going to get uglier. So, pack your bags and get out."

"You're my partner, Mack," she said. "I went into hell once without my partner, my backup. He froze up and talked himself into going back to report in instead of covering me. I swore to myself that day that I'd never do what he did. If you're going on, so am I."

She stood then and walked over to him, so much smaller, almost like a child. She took his hand in hers.

"You told me last night," he said, "that the air is rarefied up here, that small things can loom large. It might be your career you're talking about."

"Screw the career," she replied. "This is more important."

The two shared a look then, and without words everything was said. Bolan realized that finally she knew what they were up against and that it stuck in her gut as much as it stuck in his.

He looked at the computer again. "Did they check the airlines?" he asked.

She released his hand and took a breath. "Yeah. Her credit card wasn't used to buy any tickets, and her name didn't show up in any manifests. If she took a plane, she traveled under an assumed name and paid cash."

"Maybe," he said. "Have we got the authorization to get into the airlines' computers?"

She smiled. "I can get you into almost anything."

"Good. Check and see if any tickets were purchased on the *You* magazine account. I can't believe that someone hurrying to get out of town would take a chance in trying to pay cash for a ticket at the last minute if she could call it in on a credit card."

She was already moving, bringing the phone over and attaching the receiver to the modem. Within a moment, she was typing furiously while Bolan paced like a lion at the end of a tether.

"Got it!" she said after a few minutes. "Look at this."

Bolan walked behind her and stared at the screen over her shoulder. The readout showed a ticket purchased the previous day on the *You* magazine American Express account in the name of Lydia Fisher.

"The secretary," Bolan said. "And the destination...Albuquerque, New Mexico."

"And it shows that the ticket was used," Joan responded. "By a dead woman?"

"Spend another minute making sure she didn't go somewhere else after Albuquerque, and if not, check the car rental companies."

The information kept flooding in. Apparently the woman had stopped flying at Albuquerque, then had rented three cars from Avis.

"But where did she go then?" Joan asked.

"We'll worry about that when we get to New Mexico," Bolan said, moving toward the adjoining room. "Get your stuff together. We're on the move!"

7

Blocker drove the Ford LTD into the two-block stretch of shantied dust bowl the inhabitants called Trechado. He had stolen the Ford in Navajo, Arizona, just off Interstate 40 because it looked official, like something an FBI agent might drive. The car had started out a good, Republican blue, but now it was gray with dust.

It was late afternoon. The heat of the day had passed, but its memory lingered in the generated heat of the roads and buildings. Most of the inhabitants were inside for early supper, just the way Blocker had planned it. He had also planned that the sheriff and deputy would be in the office together, comparing paperwork before the shift change. Blocker had found all this out in a very illuminating conversation with Sheriff Jasper earlier that day. The man had been very excited to talk to a "big-time lawman," and had taken the promise of secrecy he had made to Blocker very seriously.

Blocker, for his part, was dressed in his best suit, his face clean-shaven, his hair neatly combed in the tiny service station just outside of town. He had debated whether or not to kill the attendant when they had stopped there, but had ultimately decided that it was better to be safe than sorry and cut the man's throat, stuffing his body in the grease rack and lowering a car on the lift to cover it.

Loreen sat beside him, wearing a severe suit, her blond wig combed down to hide her purple-and-yellow bruise. She would go in as his partner, two MAC-10s hidden in the large purse she carried. Their disguises wouldn't buy them much time, but they didn't need much.

The police station was a small one-story brick building set on a corner right in the middle of town. Its one police car, old and dirty, sat parked in front of the place. No one was on the streets. The town wasn't sleepy so much as it was catatonic.

Blocker could feel the excitement building inside him as he pulled up behind the blue-and-white squad car. This was a hell of a scam to build up, but it seemed necessary to keep the Blackman woman in place with her mouth shut.

He killed the engine and turned to Jeff and Mary Ann in the back. "Nobody goes in or out," he said. "Do what you have to do quietly."

The kids nodded, their eyes alive with excitement. Blocker looked at the woman beside him. "I want the uniforms in one piece," he said.

She smiled and opened her door, the two of them climbing out and walking right into the station. The office was small. A waiting room contained two chairs, and a half wall with a swing door separated the waiting room from the office proper, which contained two desks, one of them holding a small radio and microphone. "Wanted" posters hung on a bulletin board on the wall.

Both desks were occupied by police in tan uniforms and leather gun belts. The younger man was lean and rawboned, about Jeff's size. The older one was big, but big all around, his fleshy face squeezed into the tight collar he probably only buttoned for the FBI visit.

"You must be Sheriff Jasper," Blocker said to the fat man.

"That I am," the man said with a nasal twang. He stood and waddled over to the partition with his hand extended. "And you must be Mr. Turner from the FBI."

They shook hands all around, the younger cop getting introduced as Johnny Deatherage.

"This is my partner, Lisa Myrnick," Blocker said.

Jasper looked surprised. "I didn't know they allowed women in the Bureau."

"Welcome to the twentieth century," she returned.

"I like your place," Blocker said.

"Ah, it can't be much to a professional like yourself," Jasper replied, "but we're right proud of it."

"You have cells in back?"

"Through that door," Deatherage said. "Got a drunken cowboy and a couple of yahoos up from Roswell who couldn't keep out of fights. Big day for us."

"Any messages for me?" Blocker asked.

"Just one," Jasper said. "A woman called to verify that you were comin' and about what time."

"Nothing from Washington?" Blocker asked.

"No, sir," Jasper said. "I'd'a remembered that. I'll have to say this is about the biggest excitement we've ever had around here. To tell the truth, me and Johnny have been bustin' a gut tryin' to keep quiet about it."

"But you have kept quiet?"

"Yes, sir," the man answered. "We take our jobs serious."

"Good," Blocker said, nodding to Loreen. "Then I guess everything's set. If you gentlemen will be so kind as to take off your clothes."

"What!"

Loreen came out with a silenced stuttergun. "Quickly," she said. "Quietly."

The deputy didn't hesitate for a second, his hand going immediately for the long-barrelled .38 that rode on his hip. Loreen fired a short, quiet burst head high, blowing off the top of his skull before he even cleared leather. His body stood for a millisecond, limbs twitching, before slamming backward and sprawling across the desk.

Loreen turned back to Jasper, who stood, open-mouthed, staring at what had once been his friend. "Do it now, fat boy," she said. "Roll that jelly out of the clothes."

The man began to fumble with his clothes as Blocker hurried to the front door. He pulled it open, looked up and down the street, then motioned for Jeff to come inside.

The boy hurried in, Blocker winking to Mary Ann before closing the door.

"Get the dead one's uniform off," Blocker told Jeff. "I think you can get into it pretty well."

"Wow," Jeff said. "I get to play cop."

Blocker took the other SMG from Loreen's purse and moved through the office and into the cells in the back. No use taking any chances that something was overheard.

There were four cells, three of them occupied. One held an old, wrinkled man wearing a plaid flannel shirt who sat half asleep on the bunk. Two others were occupied by young greasers who hung on the bars, cigarettes dangling from their lips.

"Look at the dude," one of them said.

"Hey, man," the other called. "Are you our lawyer?"

Blocker just smiled at them. He brought up the SMG and put a burst through the old man first, while the other two screamed and charged around their small cells, trapped.

He dropped them quickly, silencing their mouths, and made his way back to the office. Jeff was already getting into his uniform, while Jasper had stripped to his polka-dotted boxer shorts.

"Think you can squeeze into this?" Loreen asked, holding out the large uniform.

"It'll do," Blocker responded, and hurriedly stripped out of his suit. "You're really gross," he told the policeman. "How can you let yourself go like this? Don't you have any respect for yourself?"

"I'm going to kill you for this," the man said, his face strained with anger.

"And a liar, too," Blocker observed, giving Loreen a nod.

She pulled the trigger and put a short burst into the man's gut. He frowned deeply, put his hands on his stomach and staggered around, banging against the desks before finally toppling like a big tree and lying still.

Blocker got into the uniform, folds of cloth hanging on him like the skin of a bloodhound. Loreen and Jeff both stood giggling at the sight.

Blocker shrugged sheepishly. "You can't win 'em all, right?"

BOLAN SAT looking out the window of the DC-10 as it circled the city of Albuquerque. Beside him, Joan Meredith was on the air-to-ground telephone, contacting, at Bolan's insistence, every firm in the city that offered security services.

"Okay," she was saying into the cellular phone. "Thanks very much."

She broke the connection and looked at Bolan. "I think we're barking up the wrong tree," she said.

"Are there any more?" he asked.

"A couple."

"Try them. This woman is resilient, a survivor. She's going to think of everything. Can you think of any other reason to rent three cars at the airport unless it would be to transport a number of people?"

Joan nodded and went back to work, beginning the laborious task of contacting the ground operator, working through her clearance and getting the number on line. They were landing when the call finally came up.

"Is this Industrial Security?" Joan asked. "Yes, hello. This is Joan Meredith with *You* Magazine. I believe that my boss, Pat Blackman, hired some security personnel from you yesterday. She did?"

The plane touched down, bounced and came down again. The woman shot Bolan a thumbs-up sign. "Okay," she said. "How many people did she hire? We need it for the expense account. Uh-huh. And what was the destination? That was all she said? Okay...thanks. Uh-huh, you too."

She broke the connection.

"How many?" Bolan asked.

"Ten," Joan replied.

"It's not enough. Ten rented cops won't last five minutes with those pros. And don't tell me. She didn't list her destination."

"She just said to meet her at the airport and that they would be traveling southwest."

"Great."

"You know, Mack," Meredith said. "As much trouble as we're having tracking her down, maybe Freon won't be able to find her, either."

"He'll find her," Bolan said, unhooking his seat belt and standing. "He's probably closed in on her by now. Let's go talk to the rent-a-car people."

They deplaned amid a crush of people, Joan still lugging her computer. Bolan hurried to the Avis counter in the baggage claim area.

Two women in their early twenties were working the counter.

"Did either of you work yesterday?" Bolan asked after presenting his government credentials.

"Sure," Jeri, one of the girls, told him. "We both did."

"Did a woman come in and rent three cars? She would have probably paid with a credit card from *You* Maga—"

"Pat Blackman!" the other girl, Samantha, interjected. "It was so-o-o exciting getting to meet a celebrity!"

"Great," Bolan said. "Now, do you know where she was heading?"

Both girls shook their heads. "No," Jeri said. "Our forms don't require anything like that, and we would never have been so forward as to ask."

Bolan slammed a palm down on the counter. The girls jumped, startled.

"Think, ladies," Joan pressured. "This was an exciting moment for you. What did she talk about? What did she say?"

"She seemed nervous," Samantha said. "She kept smoking cigarettes and looking at her watch. She was waiting for some men...her bodyguards, I think. There were so many. That was it except for her hassle with the porter."

"Hassle?" Bolan asked.

"Yeah," Jeri said. "One of her bags wasn't on the flight, apparently didn't make the plane change in Chicago. That happens all the time...."

"Where would she file something like that?" Bolan asked.

"At the redcap office," Jeri said, pointing across the terminal. "That door with the cutout."

Bolan was off and running before the girl finished talking. He reached the half door quickly. An old man was sitting at a desk reading a magazine.

"Did a Pat Blackman lose a bag yesterday?" Bolan asked.

"Maybe," the man said, going back to his magazine. "What business is it of yours?"

Bolan didn't have time for formalities. He reached into his pocket, came out with a fifty-dollar bill and held it up. "This is my business," he said.

The man stood, nodding. "Yes, sir," he said. "I seem to recall a real ruckus over that bag. It got hung up in Chicago but showed up last night. I called the number they gave me, but ain't nobody come and picked it up yet."

"A number?"

"Yeah," the man said. "She give me a number to call when the bag came in." He opened the desk drawer and pulled out a piece of paper from a memo pad, showing it to Bolan.

"Where's the bag?" Bolan asked, grabbing the number from him.

"It's right here," the man said, pointing to the floor. "But you can't—"

But Bolan had already shoved the door open and grabbed the suitcase. He undid the strap and worked the combination locks until the top sprang open. He turned the bag upside down in spite of the porter's protests and dumped its contents onto the floor. The bag had been filled with clothes and underwear. He sifted through it quickly but came up with nothing that pointed to a destination. He took the phone number and hurried out of the office, meeting Joan outside in the terminal.

"I've got her number," he said. "You run it down while I try to call her."

"Sure."

They found a bank of pay phones, and Joan hooked up her modem while Bolan called the number on the paper. He got a computer voice telling him that there was trouble on the line. He hung up the phone and turned to Joan.

"They've cut the lines," he said. "How's it going with you?"

"I'm clearing my authorization through the phone company now," she said. "We'll know in a minute."

Bolan forced himself to remain calm as the woman ran through her passwords. He had no idea how far he'd have been able to get without her and her ties to the world of electronics. He admired her devotion to duty.

"Got it!" she yelled, then looked around sheepishly. She pushed the button on her small printer and ran a hard copy of the information.

Bolan took the paper from her and read, "Cauble Ranch, eleven miles west of Trechado, just off Highway 36."

They hurried back to the Avis counter and picked up a road map of New Mexico, checking the location from where they were.

"A hell of a drive," Joan said. "It's already getting late."

"Not too long a flight, though," Bolan said.

She stood, putting her hands on her hips. "But where do you find a runway?" she asked.

"It's flat country," he answered. "I'm going to air freight and see what they've got. Meanwhile, you get the state police on the horn and tell them what we've got. Tell them to get in touch with the media and see if they'll broadcast a warning over the television and radio."

The man turned and strode off, Meredith watching him disappear into the crowd. He had death written all over him. She felt a chill, but it was nothing that a jacket could cure.

8

"But it's like she spends twenty-four hours a day just trying to get my goat," Jeff was saying. "She's always picking at me, always correcting me."

Blocker pushed the mirror-reflecting sunglasses a little higher on his nose, the loose sleeves of the sheriff's uniform sliding down his arms. "Look," he said, "it's natural for brothers and sisters to fight. It's the way of the world."

"But I don't like it!"

"That's the whole point, dummy. She pushes you because it gets a reaction. Whenever she makes you mad, she feels she's won." Blocker smiled at him. The kid filled the uniform pretty well. "Try this. Just ignore her. If she can't get your back up, she'll get tired of screwing around with you."

Jeff shook his head. "If I ignore her, she'll just think I'm a coward."

"There aren't any cowards in my outfit, boy. I don't want either of you to forget that. We all work together. We all think together. You were willing to shinny up that telephone pole back there to cut it, but Mary Ann suggested we just blow up the whole damned pole. You've got to admit, it was a workable idea."

Jeff leaned back, laughing. "Yeah, great idea. It almost fell over on us!"

Blocker started laughing, too. "And the whole time you were yelling, 'Timberrrr!'"

There was a honk from the LTD. Mary Ann, who was at the wheel, pointed off to the left. The man looked. A sprawling gentleman-farmer ranch sat nestled in the foothills of the Gallo Mountains a half mile distant. Up ahead, an access road cut off 36 and wound toward the main gate.

"Is the camera ready?" Blocker asked.

Jeff patted the camcorder that sat in his lap. "This will work easier than the one back in Hollywood."

"Is the ordnance handy?"

"Weapons loaded with fresh clips, extras on the floorboard."

"Okay." Blocker slowed and turned the squad car onto the access road. "Worry about the opposition first, the camera later. The woman's got ten bodyguards and at least one household servant. With luck, we'll be able to hit most of the guards before they even know who we are. Remember, nobody gets out alive."

Jeff picked up his Ingram and slipped off the safety. "Do we ice the gate guards?" he asked.

"Only if they don't let us in. We'll leave them for the ladies otherwise." He reached down and turned on the revolving lights on the roof of the car. "I've always wanted to do this," he said.

PAT BLACKMAN SAT WATCHING the evening news and wishing they'd stop talking about what was already being referred to as the Hollywood Hills Massacre.

Apparently the news media didn't have the same information the FBI had, because they still had no idea what the killings were all about. That was heartening to her. Perhaps, if they could bottle up the killers quickly enough, they wouldn't leak any more of the story to the press. She wasn't foolish enough to think they'd do that for her, but, after all, Jake Torrance *was* a presidential candidate, and that sort of scandal wouldn't look good for anybody in the government.

It seemed as if Mr. Turner should have been there already. At this point she was grateful and anxious to get into government hands. But when she had called the Trechado sheriff's office to check on the timing, the line was dead. That bothered her somewhat, but didn't seem especially noteworthy given the primitiveness of the surroundings. God, how did people live without telephones?

She was about to get up to peek through the den window when she heard footsteps pounding on the front porch. One of her bodyguards, an older man, came through the door and hurried into the den.

"I think the gov'ment people are here," he huffed, his plaid shirt rising and falling as he wheezed out breath shortened by a lifetime of unfiltered cigarettes. "Them and the Trechado sheriff just pulled up to the gates."

"Have them drive up to the house," she instructed, standing. "And get everyone together. I may be able to let you all go at this point."

"Yes'm," the man said, hurrying off.

Feeling a flood of relief, the woman hurried out of the den. If she had stayed in front of the television ten seconds longer, she would have heard the special report that cut into the national news warning her, specifically, to watch out for people coming to the ranch. As it was, the message ran twice, then returned to the national news and a story about the crack epidemic.

THE PILOT'S NAME was Bill Tomlinson, and he liked to be referred to as Wild Bill. He wore an Aussie hat with the brim turned up and had a huge walrus mustache. He handled the single engine, low-wing Piper as well as anyone Bolan knew, so the Executioner forgave him his flamboyance.

"We're over Interstate 40 right now," Tomlinson informed them, pointing to the highway beneath them. "We'll pick up 117 at San Rafael and head south, then west when we pick up Trechado."

"Isn't that kind of roundabout?" Joan asked loudly from the back seat.

The man turned and looked at her. "You're wanting me to pinpoint something for you. The road map's the best way. Don't worry. It won't take long to get there."

Bolan stared out the passenger window at the ribbon of road that snaked beneath them. "You won't have any problem landing on a road?"

Tomlinson stroked his mustache. "For what you're paying me, buddy, I'll land this crate in a swimming pool."

"And look," Bolan said. "Once you drop us, get the hell out fast."

The man narrowed his eyes. "What do you mean by that?"

"This is going to be dangerous," Meredith said. "We're federal agents after some killers."

"Naw," the man said, his eyes brightening as he looked from Meredith to Bolan. "You mean there could be some gunplay?"

Meredith nodded.

"All right!" Wild Bill yelled, and slapped his leg. "I've been taking people to fishing holes and hunting spots for more years'n I can count. I haven't done anything exciting since Nam. You just show me those sons of bitches, and I'll run 'em right into the ground for you. It'll be just like skimming rice paddies in a Huey."

Bolan looked at him hard. "This is the real thing," he said.

The man nodded. "We have to draw the line someplace," he replied, and banked south, following the twisted string that was 117.

THE POLICE CAR PASSED through the checkpoint at the Cauble Ranch with barely a blink from the minimum-wage, rented protection the woman had hired to protect her. Halfway between the checkpoint and the ranch house, Blocker slowed down so that he and Jeff could slip into their latex Richard Nixon masks.

"Well, look, Dad," Jeff said, pointing. "It looks like they're all coming out to greet us."

Blocker snorted, disgusted that such an unprofessional outfit could pass itself off as security. He caught movement in the rearview mirror. The LTD was just making its way up to the gate.

"The woman on the porch," Blocker said.

"The one with the long black hair?"

"Yeah. Save her. Take out everybody else first. Looks like they're all out there, too."

Blocker was amazed. There, standing in the open yard, were eight bodyguards with their thumbs up their butts. They all wore pistols strapped to their sides, most likely .38s, and two men were carrying shotguns. He'd want to take out the shotguns first. Those were the most dangerous weapons close in. The real problem at this point was going to be in having enough parabellums in the thirty-round clip to get them first time.

"Ready?" he whispered.

"I was born ready," Jeff responded, and he held his SMG in one hand, the camcorder in the other.

Blocker slowed the vehicle, laying his stuttergun across his lap and rolling down his window all the way. They eased into the yard, coming almost to a stop, the crowd converging on them.

"Now!" Blocker yelled, and goosed the gas pedal.

He heard Jeff scream savagely and cut loose with his Ingram in full-auto. Blocker brought up his own SMG, sighting on one of the shotgun-toting men.

Before he could get off a shot, the car plowed into two men who stood directly in its path. One of them was crushed beneath the wheels. The other man was pitched into the air.

Blocker heard Loreen and Mary Ann hammering away at the gate. As he turned the vehicle in a full circle, he got a view of the other side of the yard, where four men lay on the ground, either dead or writhing victims of Jeff's attack. He gunned the engine again and bumped over them, grinding the corpses into the dust.

A shotgun returned fire, blowing out the back window.

Jeff had finished a clip and inserted another, his eyes wide.

Blocker scanned the killing ground and saw three fleeing figures.

"Count," he told Jeff, who was reloading Blocker's weapon.

The boy looked up. "Six on the ground here," he said. "Two at the gate makes eight."

"The woman just made it to the house," Blocker said, retrieving his weapon. He hit the gas and barreled after the last two bodyguards. One was heading for the cars parked near the barn, the other, petrified, was running blindly for the safety of the foothills in the distance.

The LTD pulled abreast of Blocker, both Mary Ann and Loreen comical in their Nixon masks. Blocker sent them toward the foothills, while he cut out for the barn.

"It's a roundup!" Jeff shouted. "Yah-hooo!"

The bodyguard made the cars just as they closed in. He knelt behind a fender and fired a blast from his Remington pump shotgun.

Blocker swerved, the blast ripping into the front fender. "Don't fire!" he ordered Jeff. "We want to drive out of here in one of those cars."

He circled wide, giving the rent-a-cop plenty of time to jump behind the wheel of the Thunderbird he was using for cover. The engine roared to life, tires spinning wildly as the out-of-control vehicle fishtailed from the line and careened across the wide, open yard.

Blocker gave chase, closing quickly. As they came abreast, Jeff fired a burst from the Ingram, the body-guard's car slewing out of control.

The T-Bird flipped over, rolling three, four times. It crashed through a pasture fence, horses scattering wildly in all directions. It finally came to a stop, up-side down, in the middle of the field.

Blocker hit the brakes, the squad car skidding to a stop twenty feet from the wreck. Jeff brought up the camcorder and started to record the scene through his open window. A figure struggled in the car and, sec-onds later, crawled out.

The man was battered severely, bleeding profusely from a head wound. Jeff zoomed in for a close-up as the man tried to stand, but he fell repeatedly. His leg was broken.

"Dynamite!" Jeff exclaimed, keeping the camera trained on the pitiful sight as the man rolled in the dirt.

Blocker heard a shot in the distance and turned to see Loreen bending over the man who had run for the hills. He looked at his watch. They needed to get things moving.

"You're wasting time," he told Jeff.

The boy nodded, brought up the SMG and stut-tered a burst over the T-Bird's gas tank. The vehicle went up in a huge fireball that consumed the man on the ground and nearly reached the squad car. Blocker put his four-door in gear and drove toward the ranch house.

They pulled up at the front porch and got out of the squad car just as the LTD skidded to a stop beside them.

"She's in there with the housekeeper," Blocker said, putting another clip in the Ingram. "I don't know if they're armed. Jeff. Get over to the barn and see if they keep any gasoline there.''

Jeff smiled widely and handed the camcorder to Mary Ann, who began filming immediately. Blocker stepped in front of the camera and called out, ''Patty Blakowski, you changed your name, but you cannot escape Islamic justice! Come out now and accept our just vengeance!

''You are the second name on my list, and though you surrounded yourself with mighty protection, it was a feeble and doomed attempt to save your miserable life. The judgment of our leader, Colonel Moammar Khaddafi, a god to his people, is inescapable and you must pay with your life. You will come out now, or risk our purifying flames of righteousness.''

There was the sound of a screen door slamming. The old housekeeper had made a break for it and was running toward the hills.

Loreen gunned her down quickly as Mary Ann, giggling, filmed the action.

''We're still waiting, Patty Blakowski!'' Blocker called. He looked at his watch. They were taking too long.

Jeff had returned, lugging a five-gallon can of gasoline. Blocker took off his sheriff's shirt, unscrewed the cap from the can and fed in part of the shirt.

''Give me a hand,'' he commanded Jeff. They carried the can onto the porch, setting it near the living room window.

Blocker took a disposable lighter out of his pants pocket and set the shirt on fire.

"On three," he told Jeff. They hefted the can to waist level and began swinging it back and forth. "One...two...three!"

They tossed the huge Molotov cocktail through the window and charged off the porch. Seconds later, the camera rolling, an entire section of the house exploded in an orange fireball.

The fire raced through the wooden structure, thick black smoke billowing into the deepening twilight of the New Mexico sky. The blistering inferno was so hot on their faces that they were forced to back away.

"There she is!" yelled Mary Ann, pointing to the front door.

Pat Blackman had burst through the front door in a dead run, her head whipping back and forth like a cornered animal's. She saw them standing in the yard and veered off sharply in another direction. Loreen raised her weapon.

"No!" Blocker shouted, then to Jeff, "Get her."

"Yes, sir!" the boy responded enthusiastically. He gave chase, catching her before she'd traveled thirty yards. He brought her down with a hard tackle, then started flailing away at her and ripping her clothes off.

The others ran to catch up, Mary Ann filming the whole episode. Jeff had beaten the woman viciously, his fists pounding her face and body.

"Go little brother," Mary Ann rasped, her breath coming hard with the thrill. "Do her! Do her good!"

"Get a close-up," Blocker ordered.

"THERE!" BOLAN SAID, pointing. "Smoke."

Tomlinson banked in that direction, quickly closing distance on the Cauble Ranch. Big Thunder was in

Bolan's hand; Meredith withdrew an Uzi from her bag.

"Let's get down on it," Tomlinson said, and put the flaps down, angling sharply toward the now-visible orange flames. "Good God, look at the yard!"

Bolan looked. Bodies lay everywhere. They were too late....

"Movement!" Joan yelled, pointing a short distance beyond the burning house.

There were four of the ghouls, bent over a body like vultures picking flesh from bones. They looked up as Tomlinson swept past.

"Set it down!" Bolan shouted. "We can stop it here!"

The man turned to him, teeth clenched. "Let's get those bastards," he said, then banked sharply to get another run at the yard.

He cut the engine and coasted, bringing the plane down between a car and the burning house, smoke swirling around them.

As they passed the terrorists, braking, rolling hard, three of the four were up and running, the last remaining beside the body. Tomlinson gave the engine more juice and turned toward the fleeing terrorists.

"I'll run 'em into the ground!" Tomlinson yelled, jamming his hat farther down on his head.

"No!" Bolan ordered. "Stay out of it! You're no match—"

"The hell you say!" Tomlinson replied, and Bolan realized, too late, where the man had gotten his nickname. "We'll get 'em. We'll get 'em!"

The fourth terrorist had finally broken from the body and was running toward the barn where several vehicles were parked.

He had waited too long. As the Piper closed on him, he turned and opened on them with an SMG.

"Down!" Bolan yelled, the Piper's windshield shattering. Tomlinson put his hand to his face, and it came away bloody.

Then there was a thump. The big man looked out the window and saw that the wing had struck the terrorist in the midsection—and the man was hanging on to the wing, half on, half off.

"I can't see!" Tomlinson cried. "I'm blind!"

The terrorist dropped to the ground as Bolan tried to take the controls from the pilot. They were passing the burning house at full speed when they bumped over a body, the plane tipping over on one wheel; then they hit another. Mack Bolan's world became a crazily spinning kaleidoscope of screaming voices and tumbling bodies as the aircraft flipped over and rolled.

BLOCKER HAD REACHED the cars before he realized Jeff wasn't with them. He turned to see the boy firing at the plane, then the wing taking him out.

"Let's go! Let's go! Let's go!" he yelled, hustling the women into a beige Chevy Nova as the plane tipped end over end, a wing breaking off and spinning away like a huge top. He didn't know who was in that plane, but it wasn't on his schedule and was, therefore, as bad as it could be.

He hot-wired the car, then backed out of the parking space. "Everything out the window!" he ordered loudly. "Masks, ordnance, everything but the video!"

He powered the vehicle toward Jeff. The boy was lying in the yard, but stirring, trying to rise to his knees.

"That son of a bitch," Blocker cursed. "Why didn't he follow orders?"

"He never listens," Mary Ann said.

"Shut up!"

Blocker closed the distance, slammed on the brakes and jumped out of the car. "You bastard!" he screamed, taking him by the arm.

Jeff's face was as white as milk, pain etched deeply around his eyes and mouth.

"I hurt, Dad," he whispered. "I hurt inside."

"Can you stand?"

"Y-yeah...if you h-help me."

Blocker put the boy's arm around his shoulders and helped him up, Jeff groaning loudly as he straightened. The man looked toward the wreck of the plane. A door was opening, a man getting out slowly.

Blocker quickly got Jeff into the back seat, then took the wheel. He caught a glimpse of the figure from the plane in his sideview mirror. The man had a gun. The terrorist ditched his stuttergun, and he briefly considered going back for the big man. But he ultimately decided the odds weren't right for that.

Rolling down the window of the Nova, he tossed out the MAC-10 and touched the floorboard with the accelerator, quitting the hellground in an enveloping cover of dust.

IT TOOK SEVERAL SECONDS for the white light that had taken control of Bolan's brain to subside to a brown fuzzy version of reality punctuated by dazzling dots. His head was on fire, and he had to force his eyes to stay open.

"Joan," he called. "Joan?"

His landscape was all turned around. He was upside down on the floor, the plane itself sitting on its nose.

"Mack," she groaned in pain. "My arm...I think it's broken."

"Anything else?"

"No...no, I think I'm okay."

Bolan pulled himself up, aching all over, but everything seemed to work. Tomlinson wasn't so lucky. He was dead, his neck broken.

Bolan banged his arm up against the door and felt for the handle. It fell open hard, and he slowly emerged, sliding down what was left of the wing. His legs were shaky on the ground, his vision blurring double.

No more than two hundred feet distant, he saw a car stop and pick up the terrorist who'd gotten wrapped up in the wing. Big Thunder was gone, lost in the plane somewhere, but the Beretta was firmly niched in the webbing of his combat harness.

He pulled the gun out, trying to make his vision clear enough for him to get a shot in. If only the dots, like flashbulb pops, would stop getting in the way.

Then the car was floating in a fog of dust, rapidly moving away in skip jumps as the Executioner flashed in and out of consciousness. Only then did he give in to the blackness that beckoned.

WOULD YOU BELIEVE THESE MEN CAN HOLD YOU CAPTIVE IN YOUR OWN HOME?

MAIL THIS STICKER TODAY

WE'LL SEND YOU 4 FREE BOOKS

JUST TO PROVE IT.

See inside for details.

Discover Gold Eagle's power to keep you spellbound . . .

WITHOUT CHARGE OR OBLIGATION

Good books are hard to find. And hard men are good to find. We've got both.

Gold Eagle books are so good, so hard, so exciting that we guarantee they'll keep you riveted to your chair until their fiery conclusion.

That's because you don't just read a Gold Eagle novel . . . you *live* it.

Your blood will race as you join *Mack Bolan* and his high-powered combat squads—*Able Team*, *Phoenix Force*, *Vietnam: Ground Zero* and *SOBs*—in their relentless crusade against worldwide terror. You'll feel the pressure build page after page until the nonstop action explodes in a high-voltage climax of vengeance and retribution against mankind's most treacherous criminals.

Get 4 electrifying novels— FREE

To prove Gold Eagle delivers the most pulse-pounding, pressure-packed action reading ever published, we'll send you

4 novels— **ABSOLUTELY FREE.**

If you like them, we'll send you 6 brand-new books every other month to preview. Always before they're available in stores. Always at a hefty saving off the retail price. Always with the right to cancel and owe nothing.

As a Gold Eagle subscriber, you'll also receive . . .
- our free newsletter, AUTOMAG, with each shipment
- special books to preview free and buy at a deep discount

Get a stainless-steel pocketknife— FREE

Return the attached card today, and we'll also send you a stainless-steel, multifunction pocketknife with key chain— FREE

Like the 4 free books, it's yours to keep even if you never buy another Gold Eagle book.

RUSH YOUR ORDER TO US TODAY

9

Blocker sat calmly behind the wheel of the Nova, looking at the incredible line of headlights that snaked behind him on Highway 60 as far as he could see. Ahead, he was only ten cars from the roadblock at the Arizona state line. The roadblock had been set up for him. The only thing, though, was that they didn't know who they were looking for.

It was late, nearly midnight, an hour of their time wasted at the roadblock. After the incident at the ranch, he had gone west to Fence Lake, then cut directly south on 32, picking up 60 near Red Hill, where they had stopped and stolen new license plates and some clothes off a washline for him and Jeff. A bit farther down the road they had cleaned up in a service station rest room. They had no clothes and no weapons, but they had their IDs, including a credit card and enough cash in their pockets to get them where they needed to go. Nothing in the material left behind at the ranch would give them away; they didn't travel like that.

"Why don't you slide over here a little closer, Loreen, honey?" he said, putting his arm on the seat back.

"Why, Farley, you romantic dog, you."

The woman slid across the seat and snuggled close to Blocker, his arm going protectively around her shoulders.

He felt partially responsible for the way things had gone at the ranch. He'd have to be more careful. There was no doubt in his mind that someone was dogging his trail, and he'd have to deal with that problem before the hit on Torrance. It bothered him a little that he'd have to spend more time looking over his shoulder.

He was beginning to think his only real problem was that he might have to start thinking about doing the job with only three people, instead of four.

"How's Jeff?" he asked, looking at Mary Ann in the rearview.

"In and out," Mary Ann informed him, the barest hint of concern in her voice. "I'm afraid he won't stay conscious at the roadblock."

"No problem," Blocker said. "We'll use that. Let him sleep."

The car in front of them pulled through the barricade and Blocker pulled up without hesitation. It was a carnival of flashing squad car lights and honking horns. This was a joint effort between the New Mexico and Arizona highway patrols, and it made Blocker feel that perhaps they were concentrating all their efforts here, leaving him home free if he made it.

They'd be looking for a Nova, no doubt. He'd figured that, but he'd been afraid to take another car that would be missed, reported, then perhaps pinpoint his location. As it was, they had no idea which direction he would have taken.

He stopped in front of a cop with an upraised hand and a clipboard. While he looked the car over, another cop came to the driver's window.

"Howdy," Blocker said, rolling down the window. "Is it this hot here all the time?"

The man didn't return his smile. "Evening sir, ma'am," the man said, his fingertips touching the brim of his cap. "Can I see your identification, please?"

"You bet," Blocker said, pulling a wallet out of his back pocket. "You want to see my wife's too?"

"That won't be necessary right now, sir," the trooper said. "Would you take the license out of the wallet, please?"

"You bet," Blocker said, chuckling. "I always say that you should cooperate with a man with a gun."

"Yes, sir."

Blocker handed the man the license, which he studied under the beam of a flashlight. Meanwhile, the other cop had gone behind the car and bent down, checking the plate carefully.

"We heard a radio report. Are you looking for those terrorists?" Loreen asked, leaning down to get a look at the cop through the window.

The man smiled at her. "Yes, ma'am," he said, handing back the license.

The trooper shone the light inside the car, looking first at Loreen, then moving to the back seat. He caught Mary Ann in the beam, the girl smiling brightly at him and waving self-consciously. Then he moved the light to look at the boy.

"That's my boy, Jeff," Blocker said. "Fell asleep a while ago. You know these teenagers. They can sleep through anything."

The trooper straightened, his partner approaching to confer with him. After thirty seconds, he leaned down and looked at Blocker. "This a rental car?" he asked.

"Not anymore," Blocker said, then smiled. "Got it from the Avis used-car lot in Albuquerque when I moved to town. Get pretty good deals that way."

"How come you're driving on a Texas license if you live in New Mexico?"

Blocker shrugged. "You know what Texas is like now with the oil bust. In my line of work, I needed to get to someplace with a different economy. Anyway, this license hasn't expired yet, so I just haven't gotten around to getting it renewed."

"What is your line of work, Mr. Masters?"

"Life insurance, son. I free-lance. Interested?"

"In my line of work, Mr. Masters, I can't afford the premiums," the trooper said. He turned to the other cop, the man shrugging at him.

"Well, you have a good-looking family, Mr. Masters," the trooper said, smiling at Loreen. "Enjoy the rest of your trip. We were looking for a rented Nova, but not this one. Sorry to hold you up."

"Quite all right," Blocker said jovially, putting the car into gear. The cop idly waved them on, his eyes searching the car behind.

Blocker pulled out slowly, Loreen scooting away from him immediately, and drove onto the darkened recesses of the nearly deserted highway and freedom.

Now he'd have to think about Jeff.

"JUST GIVE ME MY CLOTHES!" Bolan demanded. "There's nothing wrong and I'm leaving."

"Get back in bed, Mr. Belasko," the nurse said. "No one leaves this hospital until he's released by his doctor. You've had a head injury."

"I'll leave when I'm damn well ready!"

"Is that any way to speak to a lady?" came a voice from the doorway.

Bolan turned to see Hal Brognola standing in the doorway, grinning.

"Did you just happen to be in the neighborhood?"

"No," Brognola admitted, moving in to sit on the bed. "Albuquerque's usually not on my rounds." He nodded to the nurse. "Dr. Doolin wants to see you. Leave the clothes."

The woman nodded and disappeared immediately.

Bolan got into his pants, then walked into the bathroom and stared into the mirror over the sink. He examined his swollen eyes and the bandage that covered the top of his head. He called back to Hal. "I want to get back on the trail before it gets cold."

"No," Brognola said, coming to stand in the bathroom doorway.

"What?"

"I said, no. You're not getting back out there to look for Freon. Something else has come up."

"What?" Bolan asked. "And where are my guns?"

"You sold the program well, Mack," Brognola said, moving back into the room and stretching out on the bed. "Everybody believes that Freon is a terrorist and that Jake Torrance is his next target. It's logical that you, then, should be placed in charge of Torrance's security. He's stumping in the California primary and refuses to come off his list of commitments. California could put him over the top for his party's nomination, and he won't pull back.''

"If I'm in the field, I could get Freon before it got that far," Bolan replied. "Where are my guns?"

"Looking for these?"

Bolan turned to see Joan in the doorway, her arm in a plaster cast, Bolan's combat harness draped over a shoulder.

"How are you?" Bolan asked, moving to take the weapons from her. "I hear they had to cut you out of the wreckage."

"Well, I'll never be able to look a pretzel in the eye again," she replied, "but basically I'm just a little the worse for wear. I'm better than Tomlinson, at any rate. I agree with Hal, by the way. If you go with Torrance you can just wait for Freon to come to you. Besides, if you don't, that leaves Trevans in charge of security."

Bolan slipped into the combat harness. "I can't do it, Hal. You know—"

"The country's gone nuts over this thing," Brognola interrupted. "We couldn't keep something like this locked up. It's all over the media. Meanwhile, Khaddafi is screaming that much louder that he's innocent. He's now blaming the U.S. government for setting this up as more disinformation to discredit him. We need you, Striker. The President personally authorized me to give you anything you need to carry this off.''

''What's the President going to do about Khaddafi?''

Hal sat up, running a hand through his thinning hair. ''What can he do? At the moment, the denials make it pretty tough to act.''

''I want Joan working with me,'' Bolan said.

''Done.''

Joan mouthed a silent thank-you to him, and he knew she wanted Freon just as bad as he did.

Bolan turned back to Hal. ''We hurt one of them. Let's check the hospitals for belly injuries. Check the morgues, too. Check the ditches. The body will be unidentified.''

''What hospitals do we check?'' Hal asked, writing on a notepad.

''You said Torrance is going to California. Check between here and there.''

''We've set up roadblocks.''

''He'll get through them.''

''Maybe he'll back off a bit now that the heat is on.''

Bolan walked up to Hal and put a hand on the man's shoulder. ''Hal, the hotter it gets, the better. He loves the audience, craves the excitement and thinks he's smarter than all of us put together. He'll go after the senator from Missouri, all right. It's just a question of where.''

Bolan started toward the door.

''Where are we going?'' Meredith asked.

''Where's Torrance right now?'' Bolan asked.

"Kansas City," Hal replied, "speaking before the VFW."

"And tomorrow?"

"San Francisco, operating out of his headquarters until the primary."

"Let's go to San Francisco." He pushed open the door, and they walked into the hallway. "I want to coordinate this through Stony Man," he said. "This terrorist can only be one out of a few. We can start tracing mercs from the bottom up and see who's where."

"Sounds like a shot in the dark," Joan said.

"It's what we've got to work with," Bolan returned.

The trio reached the nurses' station, turned the corner and came to a bank of elevators. They got an elevator right away, and as the antiseptic-smelling car descended to the lobby, Bolan unwrapped the bandages that swathed his head.

"Is that wise?" Hal asked.

"It makes a great target, doesn't it?" Bolan replied dryly.

Hal left them on the ground floor to return to pressing business in Washington. Meredith and Bolan were to fly to California the next day, so they decided to spend the night in a local motel.

Bolan was silent during the cab ride and silent as he made his way to his room, its quiet a desperately welcome friend after so much exposure to the inanities of the system.

There was a reason why he always worked alone, why he always ended up that way. It was because people could get so tied up in the things that weren't important, they could completely overlook things that were, and that enough exposure to the unimportant intricacies of the lives of others could taint even the purest person.

He lay down on the bed and put his hands over his eyes. The hell of it was, he knew that Freon thought exactly the same way as he did. That was what allowed him to operate so freely, so lawlessly, in a world that desperately sought order. The person beyond order, beyond convention, could do anything he chose to do. The person who could recognize and avoid the pettiness of the human animal could control that animal. Bolan had boiled the entire concept down to a single thought—live large.

But to Mack Bolan, that kind of freedom implied responsibility—to yourself, to the others who inhabit your world. Freon was the dark side of all that Bolan lived for.

There was a knock on the door.

Bolan rose and answered it after checking through the fisheye. She was probably the only person he would have let into his private hell at that moment, and she had earned her entry the hard way.

"I know I'm probably intruding," she said, moving past him to stand in the center of the room, "but I had to stop by anyhow."

He closed the door and returned to the bed. His head hurt, a slight dizziness never quite abating. "Have a seat," he said, indicating the chair tucked under the hotel desk.

"You're hurting, aren't you?" she asked.

"Probably no more than you are," he replied. "Thanks for the concern."

"Are you...all right with all this? I know we hardly know each other, but you seem to be a very...private person. I worry about you. As hard as you are, you strike me as incredibly fragile."

He smiled slightly. "I know I can count on you to keep my secret."

"You've been thinking about him, haven't you?" She looked at him, and her eyes were like X rays. He couldn't lie to this woman or brush past her.

"He's out there right now," the Executioner said, "thinking, planning, scheming, probably scheming about me as much as Torrance. But I *will* get him, bet on it. I've got to think just like him, to live in that head of his and think those black thoughts. That's why Brognola wanted me in on this thing. Freon's holed up tonight, just like us, licking his own wounds, planning his next phase."

"What will that be?"

"I think we may have hurt him this afternoon when we ran his bullyboy down. Hal will check the hospitals, but our Mr. Freon would never go to a hospital. He's got concerns right now about pulling his coup off with one less maniac on the team. That will give us an extra day or so to organize our defenses."

"It seems to me he'll have a pretty tough time with us being so prepared for him."

The Executioner just stared at her, and it seemed to Joan that his eyes looked a thousand years old.

10

Blocker stood beside Loreen in the lobby of the Lucky Star Motel and watched her plug quarter after quarter into the guts of the slot machine that stood there overlooking the early-evening traffic on north Las Vegas Boulevard. This one wasn't even here to be played long and hard. It was more like a trash receptacle for the change people received when paying their motel bills.

"Come on," he told her, keeping his voice low. "We've got things to do."

"Just a few more minutes," she said. "I've been milking this son of a bitch for an hour. I think it's getting ready to pay off."

People called the machines one-armed bandits and, try as he might, Blocker couldn't see the appeal. The man trusted his instincts, he trusted his intelligence and know-how. The idea of trusting blind luck was totally beyond him. To Blocker, it was just another example of how stupid people were—including Loreen.

"Come on," he said.

"Just a minute."

She plugged a quarter into the slot and reached for the handle. His hand flashed out, taking her by the wrist and squeezing.

"Come, *now*," he said, applying pressure. Her eyes widened in pain. She nodded quickly, the man leading her away from the machine and out into the hot Las Vegas night. No one in the lobby was aware that an altercation had taken place.

The desert night was clear, the gaudy blue and pink neon of the Strip just beginning to jump to life. The entire city was designed for night people like the Masters family. It wasn't unusual for vacationers to sleep in the daytime in order to gamble and see the shows at night.

"This is starting to get old, Farley," Loreen said, rubbing her sore wrist as they walked past the line of cars parked in front of pastel-colored motel doors. Dreamers stayed in places like the Lucky Star, people trapped in their circumstances who thought they could come to this oasis in the desert and strike it rich without having to do anything other than plunk down a few dollars on a green felt table.

"You don't like it, you can walk anytime, honey," he said, tipping his recently acquired cowboy hat to a pair of newlyweds leaving the one suite the motel had to offer. The Masterses had purchased new wardrobes that afternoon to replace what they'd ditched after passing through the checkpoint.

"What'd be the harm if I went into town and played a little blackjack?" she asked. "I don't ask for much."

"This is business," he said. "On your own time you do whatever you want, but on my time you'll keep a low profile. For God's sake, control yourself, Loreen. You really make me sick, you know?"

"You're not too great for my digestion, either," she replied, and they stopped in front of the adjoining rooms they had called home for the afternoon.

Blocker had driven all night to get there, taking a roundabout route that had passed through Phoenix, Arizona, where he had left the second videotape. He hadn't made a dupe, trusting that the network affiliate he had left it with would know solid gold when they saw it.

He unlocked the door, and they moved into the dark recesses of the room, which had obviously seen better days—some time in the 1950s. The television was on, broadcasting the national news, which was just beginning. Through the adjoining door, Blocker could see Mary Ann wiping Jeff's face with a washcloth as he lay, comatose, on one of the double beds.

"You goddamned son of a bitch," she was saying to him. "Why did you have to get yourself all bummed up like this? You wouldn't listen when Daddy told you to come on. No, you had to stay there beating on that bitch cause you haven't got any control over yourself. You're about the stupidest brother anyone ever had."

"Mary Ann," Blocker said, the girl looking up immediately. "Come in here and watch the news."

She rose from the bed, leaving the cloth on her brother's head. She went over and leaned against the doorway. "I don't want to watch the news," she said. "It's boring."

He patted the bed he wanted her to sit on. "Come on. You're famous."

"Do I have to?"

"Come."

She sauntered over and sat on the bed. "It's not like we're really famous," she said. "Nobody even knows who we are."

"Shh."

He turned up the volume and sat next to Mary Ann. Dan Rather's somber voice was talking about a country living in shock and a state of panic.

"Here is the latest chapter in the grisly saga that has already left twenty-six people dead and serious question marks on America's ability to defend itself against terrorism."

Then they ran the tape that Jeff and Mary Ann had shot. It was jumpy and uneven, of course, but that seemed to lend a grainy sense of urgency to the event that Blocker enjoyed despite the obvious amateurism of the cameraman. The Blakowski woman's death scene was quite effective, Mary Ann getting good close shots of her face as she went through her final agonies.

"Bitch," he heard Mary Ann whisper as the woman died, and he realized that she blamed Blakowski for Jeff's stupidity. Quaint.

After the tape, the TV showed reactions to the violence all over the country and about how ineffectual the police had been. Reporters talked to Jake Torrance's campaign coordinators, and the network showed a piece of film in which Torrance had denounced Khaddafi in 1969. Then the newscaster did a short item about the government assigning a special agent to the case.

"The agent is probably the one responsible for Jeff," he told the girl. "He's the one who messed up your brother."

"I want him," Mary Ann said. "I want him all to myself."

"We'll see if we can flush him out," Blocker replied. "I want him as bad as you do."

The big man had screwed things up already. Blocker had to adjust his plans to work without Jeff, which brought him to the next piece of business.

"You guys pack," he said when the news switched to something else. "I want to go in and have a talk with Jeff about how to proceed from here."

"We need to take him to a hospital, I think," Mary Ann said, her face lined with concern. "He's really hurt bad."

"I know," Blocker replied. "You know we'll do all we can."

"Thanks, Daddy."

He tousled her long chestnut hair. "You know I always look out for you and your brother," he said. "Now, you and Loreen load the car. We'll be leaving in a few minutes. He got up, moving through the adjoining doors, closing the one on Jeff's side.

He moved to the bed, sitting beside the boy. "Jeff," he said, shaking him. "Jeff."

The boy's eyes opened but never really connected. Dried blood caked the corners of his mouth. He took the cloth from Jeff's head and put a hand on his face. The boy was burning up with fever.

"Jeff, can you hear me?"

"D-dad?"

"It's me, son."

"Dad...I-I'm sorry I didn't listen...to you...I..."

"It's all right. Feel pretty bad, don't you?"

"I h-hurt all over. I think I n-need to go to a hospital . . . please."

"Sure, Jeff. We'll take you in a minute. You just relax now."

The boy closed his eyes, drifting back to the void he seemed to float suspended in. Blocker stood and took the pillow from the other bed, trying to remember how heavy Jeff was. The boy would be a bit of a problem to move, but he didn't see any way around it.

He returned to Jeff and sat beside him, then put the pillow over his face and pressed hard. Jeff began to fight for air, harder than Blocker thought would be possible. His whole body writhed on the bed, his arms pushing hard on the man's body.

"Damn," Blocker muttered, and threw himself over the boy's body to stop the thrashing that threatened to throw them both off the bed.

After thirty seconds, the boy's movements lost some of their intensity, reducing to spasmodic jerks. Within a minute those stopped, and Jeff lay still.

Blocker held the pillow over the boy's face for another minute just to be sure, then straightened, throwing the pillow back on the other bed. Jeff lay there openmouthed, his eyes wide in horror. He closed the boy's eyes. The mouth refused to stay closed, so he left it.

He stripped down the covers and rolled Jeff over, turning his pockets inside out, removing every shred of identity from his body. Then he went to the door and opened it slowly.

"Jeff's dead," he said in mock sadness.

"Dead?" Mary Ann repeated, while Loreen just looked at Blocker, her eyes narrowing a touch.

Mary Ann ran past Blocker and into the other room, throwing herself over the body, cursing Jeff and his stupidity, then cursing the man responsible for her brother's injuries.

Blocker looked at Loreen. "We were talking, and then he was…just gone."

"Sure," Loreen said, brushing past him to comfort Mary Ann.

Blocker followed them in, checking his watch. "It's dark," he said. "We need to think about moving down the road."

Mary Ann stared at Blocker, her face hard, no tears. "What do we do about Jeff?"

The man cocked his head. "My dear," he said, "we fix it so that Jeff doesn't get us in any trouble by dying." He pointed to the body. "This is what happens when orders aren't followed. We're going to leave him by the road somewhere down the line. The State of Nevada will take far better care of him than we ever could."

Mary Ann turned and looked at her brother once more. "Dumb bastard."

Blocker walked to the body. "Loreen, honey," he said, "why don't you go out and open the back door of the car and watch for anyone passing by. Mary Ann, you watch the inside door, and when Loreen gives you the high sign, you give it to me."

Everyone did as they were told, Blocker bending and hefting the deadweight over his shoulder with a grunt.

"It's clear," Mary Ann said from the door.

Loreen stood by the car door, motioning him forward. He hurried with his burden from the room to the car and slumped the body into the back seat, then signaled to Mary Ann.

"You get in there and keep him sitting upright," he ordered.

Blocker walked back into the motel, checking it carefully one last time to make sure nothing was left behind. Satisfied that all was taken care of, he left the room and shut the door.

Loreen was already in the passenger seat of the used car he had bought that day on his credit card, a Ford station wagon with tinted windows.

He backed out of the parking space and pulled in front of the office to check out. Then they drove off. On a quiet stretch of Highway 95, just outside Las Vegas, Blocker pulled over onto the shoulder of the road. Mary Ann pushed her brother out the side door. Then they drove on, the girl having enough room to stretch out on the back seat and nap.

BOLAN STOOD in the opening of the large security tent that sat under a palm tree in Union Square, San Francisco. It was cold, as befitted a northern California spring night. The big man reflected on the absolute insanity of scheduling an event at this pristine, 2.6 acre manicured park. It was completely out in the open and in the dead center of the city. There were hundreds of escape routes, and a sniper had easy access from any one of a thousand windows that faced the park. If anyone wanted the best possible place in the world from which to kill Jake Torrance and get away with it, Union Square would be the place.

Carl Trevans had okayed the site selection.

The candidate, in a three-piece gray suit and with his tie loosened, stood at the base of the monolith that formed the core of Union Square. Bolan knew why Torrance had wanted a rally here. The square had been the scene of many violent, pro-Union demonstrations before the Civil War, the granite monument he stood beside a paean to Admiral Dewey's victory at Manila Bay during the Spanish-American war. To Jake Torrance, beneath the peaceful serenity of the park lined with yew and boxwood beat the patriotic heart of a proud country ready to rise in defense of its own freedom. While Bolan appreciated the sentiment, he knew that beneath the square was nothing but a huge, unsecured parking garage.

To make matters worse, a pair of spotlights held Torrance in their dazzling glare, his words ringing loudly through the sound system perched on large poles near him. The senator's team had planned on thousands attending the rally, and they weren't disappointed. A monster crowd moved at will around the park, all within touching distance of the candidate if they chose to approach him. For a man on the wrong side of the cross hairs, Torrance was the most affable, easy target he'd ever seen.

A Secret Serviceman stood outside the tent, his only job to keep away the hordes of reporters wanting access to the security details, details he had no intention of letting them have.

The big man closed the flap and turned around. The tent was camp-meeting large and filled with folding tables that held field telephones and electric lanterns. Joan Meredith sat at a table, working diligently with her computer. Trevans and several other agents lounged on folding chairs, drinking coffee and talking casually.

Bolan moved to the coffee urn and filled a Styrofoam cup two-thirds full. He felt Trevans's eyes on him the whole time. Finally he turned to stare at the man.

"Something on your mind?" he said.

"Yeah, hotshot," the man returned, his smile reinforced by his friends. "Did you come out here to fix things up like you fixed them in New Mexico?"

Bolan felt no need to justify himself. "I came out here because your security is so lax a five-year-old with a pea shooter could have killed your man thirty times over."

"Yeah? I don't hear any screaming."

Bolan took a sip of the coffee. It had a bitter, metallic taste. "I'll be going over the itineraries tonight," he said. "We'll probably be changing most of everything. First, no more outside rallies. We'll start changing hotels and routes in the morning. Secrecy is going to be the key word around here, secrecy and unpredictability."

"That's crazy," Trevans said, the other men groaning. "We're professionals, not pay-as-you-go goons. We know what we're doing. Why don't you just go stir up trouble someplace else and let us do what we're paid to do?''

''I'll tell you why,'' Bolan replied, and he could hear that Joan had stopped typing and was presumably listening. ''I think the negligence you practiced here tonight borders on the criminal. I think you're running on automatic and not thinking, Carl, a perfect example of everything that's wrong with the government service system. I'm going to keep Jake Torrance alive despite you, and if you don't get on the stick, I'm going to do everything I can to get you out of this business. Clear enough?''

The man stood up quickly, his coffee spilling, seeping across the cardboard top of the table. He cocked a fist, and one of his friends jumped up to hold him back. ''You're begging for it, aren't you?'' the man said through clenched teeth.

Bolan frowned, more concerned about the dissension than the threat Trevans posed. ''Just do your job,'' he said, taking another sip of coffee, ''and stop pumping yourself up so much.''

''You just watch your back,'' Trevans threatened. ''I've told you before—''

''No more, Trevans,'' Bolan said, raising a hand. He looked at the others. ''I assume you all have duties.''

They moved off silently, filing out of the tent. Trevans backed out behind them, glaring at Bolan the whole time.

''Get rid of him quick,'' Meredith advised from where she sat at her table, plastered arm resting on the edge. "He's going to cause you grief before this is over."

Bolan looked at Trevans's seat, as if he were still sitting there. "I don't know," he said. "The man's a hothead, and he feels like he's been shut out, but we can use him. I need somebody I can leave the details to."

"Don't say I didn't warn you."

He finished his coffee. "I'm duly warned." He walked over and stood behind her, looking over her shoulder at her CRT. "Anything, yet?"

She turned to him, reaching out red-nailed fingers to scratch under the edge of her cast. "Look at the map," she said.

His eyes traveled to the map of the United States on the table. Joan had drawn a large triangle on the map whose peak was Albuquerque and whose base points were Tijuana, Mexico, and San Francisco, with the Pacific Ocean itself being the base.

"Within these quadrants," she said, "we've established contact with every hospital and every state medical examiner. Hal has made sure that any injuries or deaths that involve internal injuries are being reported to us. I can pick up incomings through my modem whenever I want. There have been some reports, but so far they don't fit our description, or the time frame is off. I'll keep after it."

He nodded, resting a hand on her shoulder. "I know it's a hassle," he said, "but so far it's the only lead we've got."

"We could be totally wrong about this," she said.

"I know."

"Anything from Stony Man?"

Bolan pulled up a chair and sat. "So far we've narrowed it down to anyone of about a dozen people," he said. "Unfortunately, in the merc business, living in the cold is a way of life. We're trying to track these men down now and eliminate them from the list. It's a big job."

"What's the point of all this?"

"I want to blow his cover wide open," he replied. "Freon's got it all over us right now because he's established an identity that lets him move around at will. If we blow that, he's just an escaped criminal on the loose. Without ID, we're even, and we really need that right now."

Loud applause from outside reached them.

"I think he's winding it up," Bolan said. "Think I'll wander outside and have a chat with Mr. Torrance. We arrived so late, I haven't had the chance to talk to him."

She nodded, returning to her keyboard. "How about a drink later?" she asked.

Bolan walked to the tent flap and turned back to her. "How about a drink *now*?" he replied, one corner of his mouth quirking upward.

He moved into the chill, mixing with the crowd, drifting toward Admiral Dewey's granite pole. Trevans's people seemed pretty well scattered around the park. The man was doing his best. But it only took one look at the huge St. Francis Hotel that faced them just across the street to know that his best wasn't quite good enough.

Even in the chill air, Torrance was sweating under the lights. He had taken his jacket off and rolled up his sleeves. Bolan walked to stand before him in the mostly appreciative crowd. He listened.

"Where I come from," the man was saying, his lean face set and sincere, "we don't tolerate bullies. We stand up to them and show them they can't push us around. If we have to, we thrash them, and if we can't thrash them singly, we get on them in a bunch. And I'll tell you why. Once you let the bully get the upper hand, once you let him get his foot in your door, he's not going to turn loose until he's drained every drop of blood from your body.

"Well, this country is being besieged by bullies right now, bullies who want to cow us the way they're cowing Europe. Instead of muscles, they've got guns. But they all use the same weapon—fear. And every time we turn the other way, every time we stay indoors afraid to go out on our own streets, every time we let them push us around without responding, we're just keying them up to do even more. You know what bullies are like, don't you?" he asked loudly.

"Yes!" the audience responded.

"I can't hear you!" he yelled.

"Yes!" the crowd thundered.

Torrance clenched his fists in front of him. "They take and take and take until we're bled dry, until we're down so low we forget what it's like to stand upright—like men!"

He was again interrupted by loud applause.

"We can lick these bullies. All we have to do is stand there and spit in their eyes. That's it. That's how simple it is. All of us, as a people, as a country, standing together to say, no more. No more! No more!''

The crowd picked up the chant, Torrance taking the opportunity to wave to the crowd and exit the monument steps, applause following him.

Bolan met him at the bottom of the steps as Trevans's people formed a tight cordon around the man. The only one they let into the circle was Jerry Pierce, Torrance's campaign manager.

"Mr. Belasko," Torrance smiled and extended his hand. "Good to see you again. Glad you could join the team."

Bolan shook hands. "You have a persuasive voice," he replied.

Torrance grimaced. "Sorry to bring the pressure down on you. I'm frankly not ready for my family to read my obituary yet, and you're an easy man to trust."

Bolan nodded. "Thanks for your honesty."

Pierce broke into the conversation. "We need to move along, Jake," he said. "The union fund-raiser starts in thirty minutes."

"All right, I—"

"Not quite yet," Bolan said. "I'd like to have a few moments with you first. We need to discuss your security."

"We can do that tomorrow," Pierce said, scowling at Bolan. "We really are on a tight schedule."

"I'm in charge of the schedule now," Bolan said.

"The devil you are!" Pierce protested loudly. "And just who do you think you are?"

Bolan could see Trevans smiling broadly from the fringes of the group.

"He's the man who's going to keep me alive long enough to get elected," Torrance said, putting an arm around his manager's shoulders. "Come on, Jerry, lighten up. If I'm late for the fund-raiser, they'll just think I got held up by hordes of adoring fans."

Pierce tightened his lips. "It's your party, Senator," he said, and Bolan was once again struck by the inability of people to see beyond the end of their own noses.

"Where do you want to talk?" Torrance asked.

Bolan looked around. The crowd hadn't dissipated. They were strolling around the park, taking their time.

"The garage," Bolan suggested. Torrance shrugged and followed him. They walked through the park with their protection, exiting at the corner of Geary and Stockton and walking down the stairs to the second level of the garage.

There was some activity in the semidarkness, people leaving the rally, some returning from shopping. Bolan picked a car that wasn't locked and opened the door.

"Your car?" Torrance asked.

"No, but it will serve just as well."

Bolan climbed behind the wheel, Torrance getting in the other side. When they closed the doors, Bolan locked them by pushing a button on the door panel.

"I'm not very diplomatic," Bolan said, "as you already know."

"And?"

"And I'm going to get right to the point. I'm not exactly crazy about the way I've been ordered here to look after you, but I'll live with it. But in exchange I want you to be straight with me." He half turned on the seat, staring at the man in the subdued light, the shadows making the senator's boyish face appear sinister.

"Anything you say," Torrance replied immediately. "Just ask."

"What's this all about?"

Bolan watched the man's face for a reaction and saw none. He was either a slick customer of the first order, or the big man was all wrong.

"What do you mean?" he asked.

"This business with the murders," Bolan stated. "It's more than just that film."

"It is?"

"The way Pat Blackman took off as soon as Seales was murdered. The fact that they're coming after you." Bolan shook his head. "There's something hanging out there just out of reach. Doesn't it strike you as odd that all three of you involved in that project went on to fame and fortune on your own?"

"Well, that's interesting, Mr. Belasko, but circumstantial. Don't condemn me because some friends of mine became famous."

"There is nothing more to this Libyan thing than a simple news story from 1969?"

The men found each other's eyes in an unwavering gaze. "We went to Libya," Torrance said. "We poked around and did a story. It caused some repercussions. I swear there is nothing more to it than that."

Bolan nodded. "Okay. That's good enough for me. Now, you'd better get to that fund-raiser before your manager breaks a blood vessel. Tomorrow I'm going to revise your schedules. You're not going to be an easy target while I'm running the show."

"I really do appreciate all this," Torrance said.

Torrance opened the door and left, his security personnel sticking like Band-Aids. Bolan got out of the car slowly, watching them disappear into the shadows. He wanted to believe the man, but something kept nagging at him, like a headache wanting to start.

He shook it off and jammed his hands into his pockets, walking back to Joan Meredith to see if the computer had come up with anything.

He wondered what Freon was doing.

11

Bolan sat at the old wooden desk in the only office in Jake Torrance's campaign headquarters and listened on the telephone to the Chief of Police tell him exactly why he couldn't give him the police protection he was asking for.

"I appreciate your problem," Chief Dodd was saying, "but we just can't commit a major section of our police force to your hunches."

"It's not a hunch," Bolan said. "These people are coming for Senator Torrance, and his blood will be on your city if you don't adequately protect him."

"You don't have any proof of that," Dodd replied. "Look Mr. Belasko. Just like every other major city in this country, we're having deep economic problems right now. Our police force is barely adequate in meeting the needs of its taxpayers. Add to that the fact that there are a number of candidates campaigning for office right now, all of whom will demand and have a right to expect the same protection that we will be giving to your candidate—"

"He's not *my* candidate," Bolan said tightly. "I'm not working for him. I have no axes to grind, I'm simply trying to protect the man."

"As I was saying," the chief went on, speaking in measured tones as though he were talking to a dull-witted person. "I'd have to give all the candidates equal protection, or they'd feel I was favoring Senator Torrance. That's the way these things go. As it is, most of the candidates think this is some stunt you people put together to use the misery these so-called terrorists have caused in order to get the senator elected."

"How many men?" Bolan asked. "How many can you give me?"

"Ten each shift," Dodd said, "and that's pushing it."

"That's not nearly enough, I—"

"This is not negotiable, Mr. Belasko," the chief replied coldly. "We've been in meetings with the mayor and city council for two days over this issue."

Bolan took a breath, resigning himself. "All right," he said. "Tell them to report to the senator's headquarters on Market Street."

"Right."

"Thanks."

"Good luck," the chief said, and hung up.

Bolan put down the phone and leaned the old executive chair back on squeaky springs. He was tired and angry. Nothing was going right. He couldn't get the people or the support he needed to give Torrance the proper protection. He had been up most of the night with a headache, but it hadn't been the pain that had kept him awake. It had been Freon.

By now the man knew that people were after him, that they were entering the cat-and-mouse stage of the confrontation. From here on it was going to be a question of who made the first, and worst, mistake. The sleepless night had been a swirl of plans and counterplans for people who didn't even begin to appreciate the immensity of what they were dealing with. Fearless, formless, unrelenting death was something most Americans never had to look in the face. Bolan was having to force open eyes that desperately wanted to stay closed.

The coffee in his cup had grown cold, the half-eaten doughnut stale before he'd ever gotten it. He stood, walked to the window that was set in the plywood wall and looked out into the bustling headquarters. Outside, on Market Street, reporters and workers jammed the sidewalk, all trying to get past the door security that Bolan had installed.

The headquarters was located at the base of Turk Avenue, where it jammed into Market, which sat at the base of the incredible hills that had made the city famous. San Francisco climbed up from Market, nearly straight up, and as Bolan stood in his cubicle he could see one of the city's ancient cable cars slowly climbing Powell, inching toward Chinatown. Market eventually ran into San Francisco Bay, just blocks from the Bay bridge to Oakland.

It brought back memories for the big man. A million years ago, early in his Mafia Wars, Bolan had brought cleansing hellfire to the San Francisco Mafia. The city was one of the most beautiful in the world, but Bolan had glimpsed the ugliness that lay beneath the surface. San Francisco had marked a major rite of passage for Bolan. The passage was different now, as he dealt with the harsh realities of the bureaucratic jungle, but the setting was still the same, the feelings not quite as intense as they battered against many years of emotional scar tissue.

He watched as Torrance moved toward him through the maze of tables and workers. The senator had Pierce in tow, and neither of them looking happy.

Bolan went back to sit in his chair. He'd been waiting for this.

The men burst through the door without knocking, Torrance throwing Bolan's revised itinerary on the already cluttered desk. "Just whose side are you on, Belasko?" he asked.

"I'm not on anybody's side," Bolan replied. "I take it you've got problems with my itinerary."

Pierce moved beside Torrance, slamming a hand down on the desk. "Don't you understand?" the man said. "The election is the day after tomorrow. If Jake can take California, he'll have the nomination wrapped up. But to take California, he's got to get out there and meet the people. He's got to have access. You've canceled every outdoor appearance on the schedule!"

Bolan's eyes flicked to the doorway. Joan Meredith stood there, trying to get his attention. After a few seconds, she wandered away.

"We can't protect you when you're outside," Bolan said. "It's as simple as that. My feeling is that if you do outdoor demonstrations over the next two days, you're a dead man."

"We've been talking to Carl Trevans," Pierce said. "The man has done an excellent job for us, and he says we have more than adequate protection for outdoor rallies.''

"Fine," Bolan said. "Then call the Justice Department and have me taken off duty."

"Let's not be hasty," Torrance told Pierce. "I've seen Mike in action. He knows his stuff."

"And what about all these changes?" Pierce asked. "What's wrong with our staying at the Hyatt Regency?"

"I don't want anyone to know any more about your whereabouts than they have to," Bolan said. "We pulled some strings and have gotten the top-floor suites at the Mark Hopkins. We're going to defend the place and not tell anyone you're staying there. It will solve a lot of problems. I would also suggest hiring more security."

"Do you think we're made of money?" Pierce shouted. "We can't afford any more security. Hell, we can't afford the changes you've already made!"

"And all the secrecy," Torrance added, "is contrary to my image. I need exposure."

"The sidewalk is jammed with reporters," Bolan said. "Go talk to them."

The phone rang, effectively silencing everyone.

"Excuse me," Bolan said, picking up the receiver. "Belasko."

"It's me," came Joan's voice. "Get rid of them. I need to talk to you."

"What's up?"

"I think we've found your body."

Bolan looked up, covering the mouthpiece. "It's the Justice Department," he said. "I've got to take it."

Pierce's face reddened. "I don't care who it is, I—"

Torrance stopped him with a hand on his shoulder. "Not now, Jerry. Mike's only doing his job. Let's leave him alone."

Pierce wiped his sweaty face. "Yeah, sure, Jake. We'll rethink this and talk later."

"Good," Bolan said, nodding as they moved out the door.

"Okay," he told Joan. "Get in here."

Within thirty seconds she had slipped in the door, locking it and pulling the shade on the window.

"God, you look awful," she said, dropping a printout on his desk. "If you don't ease up, you're not going to be in any shape to tackle Freon."

He gazed at the mass of information. "Thanks. Now, give me the high points on all this."

"I've been through a lot of reports since last night," she said, pulling up a folding chair and sitting, resting her broken arm on the desk. "Over a hundred. Some looked pretty good, but I tossed them out when I saw this one. The body was found, without identification, by the side of the road on Highway 95, just outside of Las Vegas. It's a young man, somewhere between age sixteen and early twenties. The actual cause of death is suffocation, but he was already dying when he was killed."

"Internal?"

"Massive internal injuries. I spoke to the Las Vegas M.E. myself, and he said it looked as if he had been hit extremely hard in the midsection with a long, flat object. A ruptured kidney would have killed him within hours of his murder.''

"Time of death?''

"Sometime early last evening,'' she said, taking something out of a file folder. "The Highway Patrol found him in the middle of the night.''

She tossed the object, a photo, onto the desk. "This was zapped to me this morning,'' she said. "A picture of the deceased.''

He held up the picture, studying it. The mouth was locked open in a silent scream. The eyes were being held open for the photograph. It wasn't much of a picture, but it would have to do. It was a boy, just a boy. Nothing shouted out at him, nothing made identification any simpler. He was looking at a photo of a dead kid, nothing more. Instinct would have to carry it.

"Let's go with this one,'' he said.

"Great,'' she replied. "Now that we've got it, what do we do with it?''

Bolan began to sort through the papers on his desk, looking for the sheet he had checked out and written up last night while he couldn't sleep. "If you were Freon,'' he said, "and had come to this country to establish a new identity, one that would give you cover as an American citizen, what would be one of the first things you'd want to do?''

"Given his line of work,'' she replied, "about the best thing he and his people could want would be something that would give them legitimacy and access worldwide. A valid American passport.''

Bolan pointed at her. "Bingo!" He found the list he was looking for and handed it to her. "If I were Freon, I'd get a passport first thing. Here's a list of passport agencies around the country. There are thirteen of them, but I think we can cross Honolulu off the list and bring it down to an even dozen. When you get a passport, you send two photos along to the bureau with your application. One goes in the passport, the other in the government files."

"I get it!" she said excitedly. "If we can check back through the records for the past couple of months, we might be able to match up a photo with this picture of the dead kid."

Bolan smiled tiredly. "Right. And if we can make a match there, we've probably got the line on all of them, because I'll lay odds they're traveling as a family, especially given the fact that this one is young."

"He'd use children?"

Bolan stared hard at her. "Why not?" he asked, not expecting an answer. "With some luck we might be able to expose his cover soon and flush him into the open."

She stood, holding up the photo and Bolan's list. "I'll get this out on the wire right away."

"Any problem getting agents to the locations?"

"I'll handle the red tape. We can probably lever the FBI on this one."

He nodded. "I want a copy of the photo sent to Stony Man, too. They can get to work on Freon's real identity."

Joan moved to the door, then turned to look at him. "You really think this will help?" she asked.

"It'll take him off his game plan," Bolan replied. "That sure can't hurt any. We'll start him worrying a bit."

She opened the door, still looking at him. "Take it easy, Mack," she said. "Try to maintain some distance with this."

"Yeah," he agreed, not returning her gaze. "I'll do that."

THE SILHOUETTE HAD BEEN HUNG at fifty feet down the darkened range, the only light shining dimly above the target. Blocker held the semiautomatic stiff-armed in front of him, sighting along his trigger finger the way he'd learned with his first .45 automatic.

He smiled at the weight—less than three pounds fully loaded—then squeezed off a 6-round burst, the pops muffled to a distant tick through the headgear he wore.

He lowered the weapon, satisfied at its feel. He took off his headset, resting it around his neck. "I like it," he said. "I really do."

The basement lights came up, and Juicy walked up to him, smiling. "The Glock-17's the best damned weapon being manufactured today," he said. "When you gave me the call, old buddy, I knew what you'd like."

Blocker gave the man a grin, despite his dislike for him. Juicy was a wastrel, a creature of total indulgence. Weighing in at more than three hundred pounds, the man's gut overhung his belt and bounced when he walked. His long greasy black hair was covered with a red ball cap, his straggly beard always wet with tobacco juice—hence his nickname.

But Juicy had a way with ordnance. His small, residential home three blocks off the ocean in Pacifica, California, was the West Coast crossroads for every piece of illegal artillery making its way through the country. Revolutions had been plotted from Juicy's basement-cum-firing range, quality always guaranteed. Blocker had used his weapons many times with satisfaction and had been using them since Nam.

"Let's see if you still got your eye, old buddy," Juicy said, and every time the man got familiar with him it made Blocker stiffen with contempt.

Juicy pushed the button inset in the soundproofing, and the target pulley whirred to life, quickly bringing the silhouette to them. The man ripped the target off the line and whistled in admiration.

"All six like a big hole in the head," Juicy announced. "You're still the best shooter I've ever seen."

"The weapon's a hundred percent plastic?" Blocker asked.

"You bet. Frame, trigger, grip, magazines…hell, even the holster's plastic. This thing won't even make a metal detector yawn."

"What about the bullets?" Blocker asked, his entire attention locked up in the contours of the gun.

"They're 9 mm Teflon parabellums," Juicy said, spitting a line of tobacco juice on his concrete floor. "The clip holds seventeen of 'em. I get these direct from the manufacturer in Austria."

He turned to look at Loreen, who sat just behind them, her own headgear beside her on the faded green couch. She was going through a stack of newspapers on her lap. Next to the couch, a wooden staircase rose to the main floor. The smell of mildew permeated everything.

"What do you think, Loreen?" Blocker asked.

The woman looked up, and he tossed her the gun. "I like it," she said, turning it around in her hand. "I love the weight."

"It's smooth as milk," Blocker said.

"Hey, where's the girl?" Juicy asked.

"Mary Ann?" Loreen said. "I told her it was all right to go up and watch television."

The man frowned, and he spit on the floor. "I don't want nobody going through my stuff."

"She's just watching television," Loreen said sweetly. "Isn't that all right?"

"For now," Juicy said, then looked at Blocker. "So, what do you think, old buddy?"

"Do they make silencers for these things?"

"Nope," Juicy replied, reaching into the front pocket of his low-riding, dirty pants. "But I whipped up a little something myself just for you." He pulled a three-inch silencer out of his pocket and held it up proudly. "Made outta the same stuff they use to make the gun. Cut your report down eighty-five percent."

"You're a magician," Blocker said, and took the silencer from the man. "Now, if you can materialize about six of these for me, thirty loaded magazines, twenty pounds of C-4 plastique and smoke bombs, maybe we can make you a rich man."

Juicy moved to a storage bin at the side of the basement, unlocking it with a key. He began unloading ordnance onto the floor. "I'd normally soak you for about twenty grand on this stuff," he said, grunting every time he stooped with a small case of ammo, "but, you know, money's not everything in this world. Maybe we could make a deal."

Blocker released the clip from the butt of the weapon, checked it and slammed it back in. "What kind of deal?"

Juicy wiped his mouth with the back of his hand. "You give me ten grand and the rest of the night with that sweet little thing upstairs, and you just bought yourself some hardware."

Blocker laughed, turning to look at Loreen, who was smiling widely.

"I don't see nothin' funny," the man replied angrily. "That's my deal. Take it or leave it."

Blocker put up a hand. "I'm sorry for laughing at you, *old buddy*, it's just that, you see, I wasn't intending to pay you anything."

The man's face hardened like rock. "Not funny, pal."

"I'm not much of a jokester," Blocker returned, cocking the gun. "I just can't leave any loose ends this trip."

Juicy turned and tried to run, his immense bulk shaking wildly with every step. He had nowhere to go except down his own range, and Blocker decided to try the Glock on a moving target. As with the silhouette, he aimed high and squeezed off a pattern of six that took half the man's head off before the momentum of his still-running body slammed his dead remains into the soundproofing at the end of the range. His headless body fell to the floor, limbs twitching for half a minute before finally quieting.

"It says here," Loreen said, pointing to the paper on her lap, "that a man named Belasko is in absolute charge of security at this point of Torrance's campaign."

"We're just going to have to get around him. First thing we need is access to a hotel computer. They're all netted for reservation courtesies."

"Maybe they'll move him to a private residence. They won't have to worry about other guests that way."

Blocker shook his head, leaning back on the couch. He let his head rest on the couch back for a second, then jumped up, running a hand through his hair. "This thing is filthy! Juicy was such a pig." He straightened. "Hotels are set up for feeding and sleeping a great many people easily. It's only logical, considering all the security they've probably got at this point. Plus a house isn't easily defendable. A hotel provides defence by its very size. It'll be a hotel, all right."

They heard a noise on the stairs and turned to see Mary Ann charging down, a metal box under one arm, the other hand holding a piece of rope.

"Look what I found!" She laughed, holding her hand out to Loreen.

It wasn't a rope, it was a snake, a cobra. Her fingers were locked behind the head, holding the jaws.

The woman screamed, and Mary Ann dropped the snake in her lap. Both Loreen and Blocker jumped up, the man grabbing the snake by the tail and tossing it onto the range where he took its head off with one shot from the Glock.

"You freak!" Loreen screamed at Mary Ann. "You goddamned little freak!"

"Screw you!" Mary Ann returned. "Can't you take a joke?"

Loreen jumped at her and grabbed her by the throat. The box dropped from the girl's grasp and crashed onto the floor.

"Enough!" Blocker yelled, trying to separate them. He got them apart, pushing Loreen onto the couch. She tried to jump up, but Blocker cocked a fist and shook it in front of her.

"She could have killed me," Loreen said, rubbing her arms where Blocker had grabbed her.

"But she didn't," he said, then turned to see Mary Ann giggling behind him. He whirled and slapped her hard, which brought a look of shock to her face. "Where'd you get the snake?"

Mary Ann's features relaxed into a pout, and she crossed her arms. "Why should I tell you?"

His voice softened, and he walked up to run a hand through her long hair. "Come on, honey. I'm sorry. Now tell me where you got it."

"In a footlocker in his bedroom," she said, her hand touching where she'd been slapped. "There were some smelly clothes, the snake and this box."

Blocker bent to pick up the box, using a penknife to pry off its lid. The box was full of money.

"Jackpot," Loreen said reverently. "The snake was guarding the Bank of America."

"Did I do good, Dad?" Mary Ann asked.

Blocker pulled her to him, holding her close and kissing the top of her head. "You did great, honey. I think today has been our lucky day."

12

Mack Bolan stood at the big oak and gold-fixtured front doors of the Mark Hopkins Hotel and watched the American Airlines security people install the metal detector. The hotel guests would have to walk through it in order to get onto the premises. Matthew Higgins, the manager of the hotel, stood glaring as the security arrangements were put into place despite his resentment.

"I will not have you searching my guests," Higgins said. "This was never part of our arrangement."

"We don't intend to search anybody," Bolan said, "unless they happen to be carrying unauthorized firearms. And everyone will have a chance to declare any authorized weapons before coming inside. This should inconvenience no one. The X-ray machine is set up unobtrusively near the elevator for the baggage. I don't even think people will notice."

"I hope not, Mr. Belasko," the man replied, flustered. "We cater to a very exclusive clientele. They don't take well to invasions of privacy."

Bolan nodded, listening to the man's spiel for the fifth time that day. The Mark Hopkins was, indeed, an exclusive place. Built at the crest of Nob Hill, San Francisco's most fashionable district, the hotel was a study in elegance of a time gone by. Its huge, open lobby and expensive, overstuffed furniture conveyed a quiet gentility. Customers had a choice of contemporary or Victorian decor in their rooms, and every one of the hotel's four hundred rooms provided a spectacular view of a spectacular city.

"What's the booking procedure?" Bolan asked, walking through the detector to test it. The machine buzzed loudly when he passed through.

"The Mark Hopkins books months in advance," Higgins replied, his eyes widening as Bolan pulled out his weapons and handed them to the machine attendant. "The people who will come in here for the night during your own stay probably booked their rooms six months ago."

The big man walked through the machine again. No alarm. "Good," he said, retrieving Big Thunder and the Beretta and reholstering them. "Then our real problems could only come from people visiting the bars and restaurants here, and hopefully, the detector will take care of them. Do you have any objections to our reserving one of the elevators as an express to the Top of the Mark Club, and making patrons without room keys take that with one of our people as attendant?"

The man pursed his lips. "I'll say no, right now, but reserve the right to change my mind if things don't work out."

"Fine," Bolan replied. "I'm not out to hurt your business. I only want to keep you from getting famous as an assassination scene."

"Touché," the man said quietly. "If you need anything, I'll be in my office."

Higgins wandered off, and Bolan moved out the front door and into the chilly afternoon. San Francisco spread out like a beautiful garden beneath his feet, the Bay shimmering diamonds under the sun all around it. The city had a toylike quality that he had never experienced before. It was like a giant playground for adults. A cable car relentlessly worked its way up the hill, the conveyance of choice for the city's gentry, who secluded themselves in Nob Hill's classy, tinkertoy heights.

He looked for his policemen. Rather than trying to involve them in his own complicated security procedures, Bolan preferred to secrete his ten plainclothes cops in stakeouts both inside and outside the hotel. Their only job was to keep an eye on the comings and goings at the hotel, to pass the word if anyone appeared to be casing the place.

Bolan wanted security to be so tight that it would be extremely difficult for Freon to stage the hit at the Mark Hopkins, thereby forcing him into the open at a rally or demonstration where chances of success became minimal under proper security. With decent troops and good security, he could protect Torrance through the California primary.

He moved back through the big doors, his guns setting off the detectors again. Then he moved past the registration desk toward the elevators, passing the Lower Bar, its bricked and sky-lit interior inviting enough that he had made the place off-limits to his security personnel, even when they weren't on duty.

It was early afternoon, the night's business just beginning to roll in. It was a bit of a relief for him to know the hotel had been booked up so far in advance.

He took the plush elevator up to the suites. The move from the Hyatt had been costly. The Torrance campaign had to pay nearly five thousand a night for the Mark Hopkins accommodations, plus the suite prices they were picking up at the other hotels for the hotel guests they had bumped from the Mark Hopkins. As an added security measure, Bolan had registered Torrance as Sheikh Faisel al-Saud and party, and intended to cloak all the man's comings and goings in absolute secrecy. He was beginning to build a net around the senator that was so tight, air was going to have to work to get in.

Bolan got off the elevator on ten, nodding to the Secret Serviceman who stood on guard by the door. He walked to suite 1004 and rang the bell, and Carl Trevans opened the door for him.

"Welcome. How's Wonder Boy this afternoon?"

Bolan walked past him into the command center. High-backed Victorian furniture had been pushed aside in favor of card-table modern with telephone. Agents sat all around, working, talking on the phones. Joan had her own table, where she sat keying data into her PC.

"Where is he now?" Bolan asked Trevans.

Trevans looked at his watch. "Speaking to a group of senior citizens at the Embarcadero Convention Center on the Bay," the man said, "and probably crying about the way you've emptied his coffers."

"How about security?"

"We've bulletproofed the dais and found him a safe and quiet route in and out of the place."

"Good work."

The man smiled. "My superiors called me a little while ago, wanted to know how come we were spending so much money."

"I suppose you gave them an earful?" Bolan replied, picking up a copy of the itinerary and glancing at it.

"You bet I did," the man returned. "You've been digging the hole. Least I can do is help you throw the dirt over yourself...."

"That's it!" Joan screamed from across the room. She had tossed a whole stackful of papers into the air, and they were floating down all over the room. "We've got a positive ID! An FBI man at the Houston passport office matched the pictures," she said excitedly. "And you were right. We've made the whole nest of them."

The telex next to her table began to chatter loudly, and a series of pixel-dot photos came out of the machine.

"They're traveling under the name Masters," she said. "Farley, Loreen, Jeff and Mary Ann. Jeff was sixteen, by the way, Mary Ann seventeen."

"The matchup was positive?"

"Good as gold," she replied. "Our people have already started running this thing down. Your friend, Farley, doesn't work at the place he's supposed to be working at."

Bolan ripped the photo of Farley Masters off the telex and stared at it. Using his hand, he covered the handsome face from the nose down and looked at the eyes, a chill running down his back. Freon.

"Carl!" Bolan called, "I want this info spread everywhere. The TV networks, the newspapers, the hotels—get these pictures out. Set up an 800 number through the Justice Department where people can call if they have information. I want Freon to see himself whenever he turns around. Let's get him on the run and keep him there."

"Does that mean we can drop all this other crap?" Trevans asked. "This guy's going to be running so fast now, he won't have time to breathe, much less crack our security."

"No, everything stays in place until he's caught or killed."

"Okay, people!" Trevans called to the rest of the room. "Stop the presses. We've got a news flash!"

Bolan turned to Joan, who was still smiling at him. "So far, so good," she said.

"So far," he agreed. "I want you to get these photos to Stony Man. Kurtzman can probably fix us up with a real ID on Freon."

"You got it," she said, then cocked her head and stared at him. "Why don't you seem overjoyed? This was what you wanted, right?"

He took a breath. "It's not only what we wanted, but what we had to have," he said. "Unfortunately Freon's now got his back to the wall. He's cornered like an animal and will fight the same way."

He turned and walked away, his elation only momentary. Now he was back inside Freon's brain. What would the man do now? Where would he go? And when he fell how many would fall with him?

"...HIS REAL NAME UNKNOWN, is traveling under the alias of Farley Masters, his identity established with credit cards and a valid Texas driver's license. A nationwide manhunt is under way, though the search is centering in California."

"They've made us, Blocker! Don't you understand that?" Loreen was loud, nearly screaming.

"Shut up," Blocker said quietly, gazing intently at the pictures of him and the others that were on the television screen. "And I told you not to use my name."

"What difference does it make now? God, we've got the entire United States of America looking for us. What are we going to do?"

"First, you're going to shut up and let me think this out," Blocker returned, voice calm. The television newsman was still talking.

"...largely the work of security chief Mike Belasko."

"We've just added a fourth name to the list," Blocker said, feeling a sudden surge of confidence and strength. He looked at Mary Ann, who was watching the TV with them. "You still want the man who killed your brother?"

She looked at him with the idealistic eyes of youth. "You still think we can get him?"

"I know we can."

The girl smiled a cat's smile. "I'd tear him apart with my teeth," she replied.

"You're both crazy," Loreen said wildly. "I hired on so I could live to spend that ten mil."

"We can do it," the man soothed. "I've got a few ideas. And besides, the last place they'd look for us would be close to the source."

"What about the colonel's contacts here in California?" Loreen asked. "Maybe they could hide us."

"They'd love to hear from us," Blocker said. "At this point in time, we're too hot, and the President isn't buying his denials. The colonel undoubtedly has put out the word on us already. We'd be dead inside of a minute if we contacted his people. In fact, that was probably his plan from the first."

The woman sat on the bed, head in hands. "We're caught then...dead."

Blocker walked over and took her by the hands, raising her to her feet. "The water's a little hot," he said, "but whoever said life would be easy? Trust me. If you don't, *I'll* kill you." He smiled sweetly, then kissed her on the cheek. "Now, let's start in the motel office. If the deskman saw us and the television report, we're going to need to take care of it."

Confusion showed on the woman's face for a matter of seconds, but her options were so limited she really had no decision to make. She nodded. "Thorough but not careless," she said.

Blocker winked at her. "That's the ticket. We're playing hardball now."

They filed out of the room and into the cool San Francisco night. They were in a decent motel in the

Fort Mason area, just off Beach Street. Blocker was thinking of Belasko as they moved toward the lobby-registration area. The man had done his best to ruin everything, but he wasn't going to get away with it anymore. He had to try to think like a top security man, then outmaneuver him. They'd find out about any hotel changes, then go underground and plan.

The lobby was relatively quiet. A maid vacuumed the checkerboard carpet while the deskman went through the registrations on his computer, his face lined with concern. A Cadillac had just pulled up under the carport. The driver got out to check in, while a woman with two poodles waited in the passenger seat.

They approached the door quickly, Blocker tapping Mary Ann on the shoulder. "Car," he said as he and Loreen pushed their way inside the small, tasteful lobby.

They shared a look. "I'll chat with the deskman," he said as Loreen reached into her purse, face expressionless. And for all her histrionics and bad habits, this was why Blocker used the woman on missions. She could take care of business quickly and efficiently when necessary.

As Blocker approached the desk, the clerk jumped up, his mouth open, and tried to run into the office behind him. Blocker vaulted the desk, grabbed the man from behind and threw him to the floor. He stuck the Glock in his neck. "I need a few minutes of your time," Blocker said casually.

"Over there!" he heard Loreen say as she herded the maid and the customer behind the counter.

Blocker pulled the man to his feet. "Let's lock up," he suggested as Loreen dropped the hammer on her two captives. The maid died quickly and quietly; the man was a different story. He began to scream and tried to run away. Loreen had to shoot him four times to bring him down, then he lay on the floor, kicking and screaming for help until she silenced him, finally, with a bullet in the head.

As Blocker and the deskman reached the doors, he could see Mary Ann in the driver's seat, pulling out of the carport to park the car. There was a large splotch of blood on the passenger window, but Mary Ann was already rolling it down with the power control on her side. The dogs were no longer yipping.

"I...I..." The desk clerk was nearly out of control, his hand shaking so he couldn't lock the door. Blocker took the key from him and did it himself, instructing Loreen to make a sign that read Back In Fifteen Minutes.

"We're going back to your office," Blocker said. "Don't worry. I'm not going to hurt you if you help me."

The man's thin lips were vibrating, his eyes desperately searching Blocker's. "P-please. D-don't... don't..."

Blocker hurried him across the floor and behind the desk, nearly tripping over the bodies that lay there. "I know it seems crass what we did, but believe me, it was only to buy us the time to speak with you. I've no reason to kill you. They already know who I am."

"I w-won't tell them a-anything," the man stuttered.

"I know you won't," Blocker said, and moved the man into the office, closing the door.

Mary Ann had gone back to the room to pack their things and load the car. Within ten minutes she had finished and pulled up to the carport, the engine running. At least now that Jeff was dead she got to do a lot more of the driving.

Blocker came out of the office within another ten minutes, a smile on his face.

"Let's get out of here," he said as he and Loreen ran toward the front door.

"Any luck?" she asked.

"Some," he replied, turning the key that he'd left in the lock. "I'll tell you about it in the car."

They moved out, Blocker getting in beside Mary Ann, Loreen taking the back. "Drive slowly down Beach Street," he said. "Let's look for a nice bar. Not a hole, Mary Ann. I want a half-decent place."

Mary Ann pulled out of the motel lot and headed toward Beach. Blocker turned sideways so he could address Loreen. "Torrance checked out of his hotel, just like I said he would," the man informed her. "And, as I suspected, he didn't check in anywhere. But my friend Mr. Kippler kept looking and found that all the people who had checked into the Hyatt in his place had been relocated from the Mark Hopkins. The records showed some sheikh or something checking in, but I don't believe it. I also got our names completely zapped from the motel's computers. Kippler was a real whiz. I was almost sorry to do him."

"If Belasko's going to this kind of trouble," Loreen said, "you can bet he isn't going to make it easy to get into the Mark Hopkins."

"Not to worry. All it takes is a little creative thought."

"What about that one?" Mary Ann asked, slowing in traffic and pointing to a small bar called the Blue Note, which was located between two fancy restaurants.

"Good," Blocker said. "Pull over."

Mary Ann found a parking spot across from the Blue Note. Blocker reached into his pocket and pulled out a piece of paper, handing it to Loreen.

"Memorize the names on this paper," he said.

"John and Esther Migliazzo?" Loreen asked.

"Right. They are our salvation."

"How...?"

"Later," Blocker said, straightening his tie. He pulled down the passenger sun screen and checked his hair in the mirror attached there. "How do I look?"

"*I* should look so good," Loreen replied. "Where do you want us?"

"Wait here," he said. "When you see me come out, follow. We'll at least get off the streets for the night and have access to a phone."

He slipped out of the car and hurried across the street against the traffic. He didn't like bars or drinking at all, but places like this were catchalls for people unattached and lonely. Bars drew them like a magnet where they then hung, suspended, waiting for a negative ion to break the bonding and take them out of the place. Blocker, when given to fancy, had thought that the existence of bars was nearly proof of the existence of God, a God who would plant these magnetic poles here for him to use.

He walked up to the building, and entered under the big blue neon sign formed in the shape of a musical note. The place was a piano bar. An old black bluesman was earning room, board and booze money by pushing on the ivories. It was dark and glitzy the way only cheap bars could be dark and glitzy. Its red vinyl booths, though, were still in one piece, so business was probably good.

He surveyed the territory through the smoke. Three unattached women were magnetized in different places, but he found himself drawn to a leggy one with short black hair and a real fetish for the olive in her martini. He decided to go with the feeling and moved toward her, taking the stool two spots away so she wouldn't feel threatened.

Out of the corner of his eye he saw the woman look at him, then return her attention to her drink. When he knew she wasn't watching, he gave her the once-over, deciding she was a hard case, one who thought herself above a bar pickup, but who was, nevertheless, looking despite herself. It was kind of like panning for gold in a sewer. He decided to be a nugget.

The bartender approached him and raised his eyebrows. "I'll have a...ginger ale," he said.

The bartender departed nonjudgmentally, but he caught the woman shaking her head and smiling.

"Did I...did I say something funny?" he asked.

She looked at him as if he were a block of granite. "I just can't figure out why anybody would come into a bar if they're not drinking," she said.

Blocker looked sheepish. "I guess it does make me appear kind of foolish," he said, staring at the floor.

"Not foolish," the woman responded. "I just don't understand."

"It's not a big mystery. I'm one of those unfortunate people who happens to be allergic to alcohol. The last time I tried to drink was ten years ago. I spent two months in the hospital. It has no attraction for me."

"But why come to a bar?"

Blocker shrugged. "No mystery there, either," he replied. "I'm a free-lance writer by trade and do all my work at home. I've lived in San Francisco for over a year and don't know anyone by their first name. The only time I met my neighbor was when he screamed at me to turn down my television. I don't go to church or to the spa, so I never get to talk to people. Tonight I was so damned lonely I began talking to myself to hear a human voice. That's when I decided I'd better go somewhere and meet a human being or they were going to take me away."

"What do you write?" she asked.

"Literary stuff, mostly," he said, smiling boyishly. "The kind that goes in small magazines that nobody reads. I could do other stuff, but I don't want to...sell out, you know."

He abruptly turned to his ginger ale. "I'm sorry. I know I'm boring you to death talking about myself. I'll leave you alone. I'm sure you don't need—"

"Not at all," she said. "It's nice to meet a real person in this place." She reached out a red-nailed hand. "And my first name's Olivia. There, you know somebody now."

He took her hand, caressing it gently. "Hi," he said, looking deeply into her eyes. "My name's Mark. Mark Hopkins, like in the hotel."

BOLAN SAT STARING OUT the suite window at the colored lights of the city far below. The telephone receiver was cradled on his shoulder as he removed the plastic wrap from a sandwich, the first food he'd had all day. "Blocker?" he said. "That's the only name you've got on him?"

"That's all *anybody's* got on him," Aaron Kurtzman said over the line. "And that's just the name he uses the most. The story we get is that he's an American who deserted the marines in Nam in 1970 and then started free-lancing. The kids are apparently his. He bought them when they were babies."

"Great. Anything anybody can tell us on him?"

"He's jobbed it around—IRA, ETA, Red Army Brigade. His latest steady work has come from the Tamil Separatists in Sri Lanka. People we know who've worked with him say he's methodical and sometimes brilliant strategically. He's a cold fish, this one. They say he's the guy who cut off J. Paul Getty's grandson's ear and the man who invented IRA 'kneecapping' to cripple people. Guys who have worked with him usually don't come back for more."

"Why, is he sloppy?"

"Just the opposite," Kurtzman said on a sigh. "He demands too much of himself and his people. They say he's never failed in a mission, Mack. *Never.*"

"Until now," Bolan replied.

"Don't start believing your own PR," Kurtzman returned dryly. "This is one tough so-and-so. Run him right into the ground before you let off. And Mack..."

"Yeah?"

"You may as well know...he's worked for the U.S. government before, in Central America in the seventies."

Bolan sat up straight. "In what capacity?" he asked, knowing the answer.

"He was sanctioned. He killed people."

Bolan ran a weary hand through his hair. "You sure know how to ruin a day, my friend," he said.

"Don't let him get away, Mack," Kurtzman urged, his voice intense. "Nail him quick, before he nails you."

"Mack!" called a voice from the suite bedroom. "You'd better get in here!"

"Gotta go," the Executioner said, standing, tense, his mind now totally cleared. "Thanks for the intel."

"We'll keep you posted on any updates."

Bolan dropped the receiver back in the cradle and walked quickly into the bedroom. Off-duty agents were relaxing on the canopied four-poster 'and the vanity chairs. Room service trays full of half-eaten food were scattered everywhere. They were watching the television.

It was an all-too-familiar scene—multiple ambulances taking bodies away to morgue refrigerators. He listened to the announcer.

"...money was still left in the cash register. Police are baffled by the brutal slayings and can suggest no motive in the case. Apparently a gunman or gunmen came into the motel lobby, slew three people inside, then went out to a car parked nearby and shot another woman and two pet dogs..."

"He's in San Francisco," Bolan said. "He's probably cleared his name from the register by now. Why wasn't I notified?"

"People don't automatically connect all this up," one of the agents said. "Are *you* sure that it's him?"

"He was staying at that motel," Bolan said, then turned to an agent named Sheldon who was lying on the bed. "Get the police on the line!" The man jumped, and Bolan kept talking. "When the ID went out over the air, he killed everyone in the lobby. Sheldon! Have the police check the register or the charge slips just in case, then tell them to seal off the roads leading out of the city. Where's Torrance right now?"

"Having a five hundred a plate dinner with the senator from California," another agent, Herrod, said. "Trevans is running the show."

"Get a call through to him and tell him to keep on his toes just in case."

"They want to talk to you!" Sheldon called from the living area.

"Yeah," Bolan said, walking out of the bedroom, knowing that his efforts to catch Freon running were doomed to failure. There was only going to be one way to stop the man—head-to-head confrontation.

BLOCKER MADE "LOVE" to the woman slowly, with care and precision, bringing her maddingly to a peak of passion time after time, only to let her subside to start the roller coaster ride all over again.

He worked her like a musical instrument until he had cracked her tough facade and revealed the frightened child beneath. Only then did he bring her all the way to the mountaintop. And as she was screaming her release and pleasure, he wrapped his powerful hands around her throat and strangled her to death, crushing her larynx as her eyes widened in horror and understanding. The pulse under his fingers fluttered wildly and finally stopped.

He got up and looked at his watch. It was 11:00 p.m. Not too bad. There was still plenty of night left.

He slipped on his pants and hurried across the rust-colored shag carpet of her chic Lombard Street house. He opened the door. Loreen and Mary Ann were already on the porch. Beyond them, the street was crooked like a snake, each curve alive with flowers and shrubs.

"Sure as hell took your time," Loreen said.

"I'm an artist," Blocker replied, checking to make sure no one was watching them enter the house. He closed and locked the door behind them.

"I'm starving," Mary Ann said.

"Try the kitchen," Blocker suggested, pointing her in the right direction. "Why don't you look for a phone book, Loreen, while I clear the bed."

He moved back to the bedroom and turned on the light. The woman looked like some kind of broken doll lying there with her head bent crookedly to one side and her eyes so wide. Dumb bitch. People were so stupidly trusting.

"How long have we got here?" Loreen called from the living room.

"She's an advertising executive," he called back to her as he walked to the closet. "She'll be missed tomorrow, so we'll need to get out early."

He opened a door to find a bathroom. He tried another and found a roomy walk-in closet. Just right. He walked back to the bed and picked up the dead-weight, carrying it to the closet and dropping it on the floor.

Blocker closed the closet door and walked back into the living room. Loreen had taken off her shoes and was making herself comfortable on the couch, a phone book on her lap. Mary Ann came out of the kitchen with a bowl of ice cream.

"What have you got there?" Blocker asked her.

"Chocolate ice cream," she responded.

"No way," he said. "You march right back in there and find yourself some real food. If you eat a decent dinner, then you can have ice cream."

"Oh, Dad!"

"Do it."

The girl frowned deeply and left the room. Loreen held up the book. "Who do you want to call?"

He sat beside her. "Remember the Migliazzos?" he asked. "Well, they're from Garden View, New Jersey, and they have a reservation at the Mark Hopkins

Hotel for three nights and two days and will be arriving tomorrow, late morning."

"So?"

"So I want to call the airlines and find out what flights arrive tomorrow from New Jersey in the late morning. I think it's time we got to know the Migliazzos...and their daughter, whatever her name is. I think it's time we became their close, personal friends."

Loreen patted him on the leg. "Farley, honey, I believe I'm beginning to understand you."

"That's not all," the man said, standing, trying to look around the doorframes to see what Mary Ann was doing in the kitchen. "I believe I'm going to make a little call to the colonel's connections."

"I thought you said they were dangerous to us?"

"They are," Blocker answered, and had a laugh at his own joke.

13

As he dragged the razor across his face, Bolan could barely recognize the tired-looking man who stared back at him from the mirror. The lines were hard around the mouth and eyes, the shell of his face brittle, cracking, wanting to let all the built-up poisons of a hundred wars in a hundred dirty places come spilling out. He hated Freon, hated the man for what he made him do to himself. Soldiers weren't supposed to think; they were supposed to knee-jerk, action to reaction, all righteous muscle and pure heart.

"Ouch!"

"What's wrong?" Joan Meredith asked, hurrying to the open bathroom door.

Bolan was leaning against the sink, breathing hard. "I just cut my damned face shaving," he said, watching the thick red drops fall to splotch in the basin. "I'm letting this thing get to me."

"Take it easy, Mack," she said. "Calm down."

"How can I calm down?" he asked through clenched teeth. "People are dying because of Freon, and the police refuse to accept his part in those murders last night. They won't put up roadblocks. The man I'm supposed to be protecting is sitting in there right now waiting to chop my head off."

"Mack, I—"

"Meanwhile, Freon is out there right now planning deaths that could be averted if people would only open their eyes."

There was a knock on the bedroom door. "Everything all right in there?" Trevans called through the closed door.

"Fine," Joan called back. "We'll be out in a moment."

"Tell Mike his eggs Benedict is getting cold."

"Mack, it'll come together. He'll leave a clue, screw up. You've got to try to step back. I'm watching this thing tear you apart."

"You don't understand," he said.

"You're dedicated," she told him, "and frustrated. You're a warrior in a totally unfamiliar war. You can't be all things to all people, Mack. You'll just go crazy trying. When's the last time you had any sleep?"

"Look, somebody's got to—"

"When?"

He took a breath and turned away from the mirror. "I haven't been to sleep much since I woke up in that hospital in Albuquerque. I can't get Freon out of my mind."

"I'll bet that he's slept," she said, her voice hard. "I'll bet he's rested as he can be."

Bolan went back to his shaving. "You're telling me that I can't control it all."

"The world's not going to hold you responsible for what happens when people don't listen to you. And if they do, so what? You know what's right. All you can do is tell people. You're a good man, but you can't force your goodness on everyone else. It just won't work that way.''

He looked, really looked, at her face. He'd been so wrapped up in Freon that he hadn't taken the time to notice her beautiful pixie face, which was now marred by concern, concern for him.

''You've got backup here, Mack. You've got Hal.'' She looked at the floor and spoke very softly. ''You've got me. We're here to help.''

He took her in his arms then, folded her close and shared a moment of peace, tranquility. Over Joan's shoulder he looked into the tired eyes of the man staring back, and wondered where Freon was.

BLOCKER STARED INTO THE MIRROR, checking the job he'd done graying his hair with the frosting perm he'd found in Olivia's medicine cabinet. The woman may have oozed an air of self-contained confidence and aloofness, but he had pegged her right; her cabinets had been virtually bursting with various products designed to change one's appearance in order to appeal to others. She'd been as scared of life as a little rabbit. Just like the rest of them. Just like all of them.

He stepped back a pace and took a good look. He'd shaved himself bald on the top of his head, leaving just the fringes of hair to color. He'd used eye shadow to good advantage by lightly accenting beneath his eyes and along the natural wrinkle lines of his face to add twenty years to his age. Small wads of cloth between lips and gum puffed out the front of his face and changed his appearance considerably. He completed the disguise by putting on a pair of weak reading glasses he'd found by the woman's bedside. Perfect— and highly workable without constant attention.

Blocker was practicing walking with a slight stoop when the phone rang. Loreen stuck her head in through the open door.

"What do I do?" she asked.

"Nothing," he said. "That's her work calling. We'll need to be out of here soon."

"You look good," she said.

He smiled. "You, too."

Loreen had taken the classic approach to aging. She'd found a red wig among Olivia's belongings. She'd then proceeded to apply a thick mat of make-up, highlighting her cheeks with a great deal of rouge and adding bright red lipstick to her mouth. Her heavily made-up face covered the remnants of her brush with Lydia Fisher's baseball bat. Keeping her lips pursed gave her mouth wrinkles. Loreen had been an actress in her early years. The role was important to her, and she took it on with gusto.

"We need to think about retiring, John," she said feebly. "I'm getting too old for this."

"Esther, my love," he replied, "if I retired, that daughter of yours would run us out of house and home."

"You call me, dudes?" called Mary Ann's voice from the next room.

They joined her, the phone still ringing, as she bopped around the living room carrying a ghetto blaster on her shoulder turned up loud.

Mary Ann had been easy. They'd simply punked her out with multicolored hair spiked with styling gel and bright purple eye shadow with sparkles. She'd put safety pins through her pierced ears and wore some baggy clothes from Olivia's wardrobe. They didn't have a name for her yet. That would come, hopefully, soon.

The phone stopped ringing, but started again within a minute. They really wanted the woman.

"We need to go," Blocker said in his old man's voice. "We'll take her car and pick up some other license plates along the way. Has everybody eaten? Time is becoming important. We may not get near food again for a while, so make sure you've got enough in you for now. I'm going to check out the place.

As was his custom, Blocker did one final sweep of the house, making sure they weren't leaving anything behind that could point to their destination or intent. The bathroom was a mess, with bottles and boxes everywhere. He decided to leave it that way, but at the last minute hurriedly cleaned it up so no one would suspect they had disguised themselves.

He looked at his watch. It was 10:00 a.m., an hour before the Migliazzo's plane was due to arrive. He'd already checked the car rental places and found that his victim was renting a Hertz car, a Cougar. That sounded good to Blocker. They would wait until the car was rented before they made their move.

"THIS ISN'T EASY FOR ME, Mike," Jake Torrance was saying. "I like and respect you, but I just can't work with you like this."

Bolan sat at breakfast with the senator and his wrecking crew, everyone trying to talk civilized over their melon and English muffins as the San Francisco morning came up bright and clear.

"You've gone nuts with this," Jerry Pierce said. "Yeah, I know, Jake says you're a nice guy and all, but this is out of control. We're talking politics here, and it has its own rules, its own way of doing things, that you just don't understand."

"I think I understand adequately," Bolan said calmly. "You think the security measures I've implemented are too severe and are interfering with Jake's chances of winning the primary."

"Hallelujah!" Pierce shouted, raising his hands to the heavens. "The light dawns! Welcome to the real world, pal."

"There's no need to be sarcastic, Jerry," Torrance said, looking apologetically at Bolan. "What Jerry's trying to say is that we've been too constrained, more so than is warranted. God, the cleaner with my suit couldn't even get in yesterday."

"Because your people refused to follow the security procedure," Bolan replied.

"Because it was stupid," Trevans said through a mouthful of coffee. Bolan turned and stared at him. Trevans wiped his mouth on his napkin. "You're a showboat, Belasko. You've become obsessed with this damned conspiracy theory of yours, and it clouds your judgment on all levels. You're not interested in protecting Mr. Torrance. All you want to do is get some points for being the man to stop the terrorists. It's not fair and it's not right, and it's going to have to stop."

Bolan sipped his coffee. "I assume that you gentlemen feel the same way," he said, putting down the cup.

"Yes, we do," Torrance agreed, not willing to meet Bolan's eyes. "Will you back off voluntarily?"

"No, sir, I will not," Bolan replied.

Torrance threw down his linen napkin and stood, turning to stare out the window. "Oh, Mike," he said. "Why do you make this so difficult?" He turned and shook his head in Bolan's direction. "We're so much alike and yet so at odds over this. It's my life, don't you understand that? My decision on how protected I need to be. You say you believe in freedom, but then try to take my rights away from me. I must get out and meet the folks or I'm going to lose this election. I must win the election to put forth the programs that are so important to *both* of us."

"I can only do what I think is right," Bolan replied.

Torrance leaned on the table. "And I can only do what I think is right," he said angrily. "You're fired, Belasko. I don't want you anymore. Just pack it in and get out of here. Mr. Trevans can handle my security just fine."

Bolan looked at Trevans. The man had a self-satisfied smile on his face, like the cat who had eaten the canary. Bolan smiled back.

"So," the big man said. "Are all of you finished now?"

The three men stared at him.

"Good," Bolan said. "Then I'll have my say."

"You have no say," Trevans growled, standing. "The senator asked you nicely to get out. Now, I'm telling you."

"Sit down, Carl," Bolan said calmly.

"Let him talk," Torrance ordered, glancing at his watch. "But we don't have much time."

"I don't need much. First of all, Carl is right in one thing he says. I *don't* really care about you, Mr. Torrance. I'm sorry to say it, but it's the truth. To me, the search for Freon is the single most important act that has taken place in this country since the Cuban missile crisis. War has been declared on our shores, and if it isn't stopped immediately, it will escalate. This is a force beyond people, Senator, and certainly beyond an election. If you really believed the doctrines you preach, I think you'd understand that.

"And I want to say that you and I are not alike, Senator. We're not alike at all. Your purpose in life is to get yourself elected President, period. I don't really think you care that much about anything else or you would have cooperated more with me on this. You believe what Carl tells you because it's the single most expedient thing connected with you getting elected. Simple. Have you ever considered that people accuse others of what they're guilty of themselves? Have you considered how much Carl Trevans has become obsessed with the idea of getting rid of me, the man who replaced him—to the extent that he would tell you anything to make me and my policies look bad? But this isn't a major point to me. You believe what Carl tells you because you want to."

He looked at Jerry Pierce. "And how big a feather in your cap is it if your boy gets elected President of the United States? Wouldn't that be worth a little risk?"

Bolan smiled, standing, feeling the great calm overtaking him. Through two sleepless nights and continuous aggravations, he was finally beginning to sort through his own mind and feelings with crystal clarity. "You know, I'm the only person here without any axes to grind. All of you are *real* busy chopping one another to pieces for the sake of your own egos."

He moved away from the table. "I've been knocking myself out to keep you alive, but right now I think I'm going to back off. On the subject of your firing me, Jake—I don't work for you. I'm helping out a friend in the Justice Department. So, until I get the official word that I'm being removed from the position, I retain full control. Perhaps one day, Jake, you'll be able to look at my keeping you alive as a kindness far above any you've ever performed in your own selfish life."

Bolan walked into the bedroom and lay down on the canopied bed, feeling better than he had in days, and slipped immediately into a deep and dreamless sleep.

BLOCKER COULDN'T HELP but chuckle when he saw John Migliazzo get off the plane from New Jersey— the man was bald, just like him. The resemblance ended there, however, as the real Migliazzo was dumpy and fat, his wife a horse of a woman with a broad, expressionless face and close-set eyes. The daughter, who looked to be in her twenties, was also large, what people politely called big-boned, and Blocker doubted if she'd ever known a man in her life. They were pigs; he'd enjoy doing them.

He tagged along after them at a safe distance, watching as they moved through the baggage check, then on to the Hertz counter. As the man went through the final preparations for renting a car, Blocker slipped away to the courtesy booth and asked to have Migliazzo paged.

There was a certain sense of authority that went along with airport paging, as if it was somehow connected to the life-and-death maneuverings of flying. It wasn't, of course. Any human being could page any other human being whenever he chose. Anyone who thought otherwise deserved everything he got.

As the friendly male authoritative voice was calling John Migliazzo to the courtesy booth for the fifth time, the little man came hobbling up, out of breath, his eyes fearful.

He walked directly up to Blocker, looking around nervously. "I was told...to...meet someone here, I—"

"Are you John Migliazzo?" Blocker asked in his older man's voice.

"Yes, I am, but—"

"I'm Jason Edwards, Mr. Migliazzo, SFPD. I'm afraid I've got some bad news for you." Blocker reached into his pocket and pulled out a folded piece of paper. He opened it slowly, methodically.

The man was shaking, confusion in his eyes. "I don't understand, I—"

"Do you own a house at—" he read from the paper "—427 Berton Street, Garden View, New Jer—"

"Yes, I do!"

"I'm afraid it burned down in your absence, Mr. Migliazzo."

The man slumped visibly. "Oh, God, no," he whined. "How did you . . . Did they tell you at the office where I'd be?"

"Yes, sir."

"Is it a total loss, or partly damaged, or—"

"I'm sorry, sir," Blocker interrupted. "There seems to be some doubt as to the circumstances of the fire, and we're going to need to take a statement from you down at headquarters."

"A statement!"

"Just routine, I assure you." Blocker clamped a hand on the man's arm, just tight enough to give the illusion of control. "You can contact your insurance man and your office from headquarters."

"B-but I've just rented a car. My wife and daughter are waiting for me."

"Ah." Blocker thought for a minute. "How about this? We'll go get your rental car and we'll drive to the station in it. Then, when you're finished, you can undoubtedly go about your business."

"You don't have to drive with me," the man said, noticing for the first time the pressure on his arm. "I'll follow you."

"I'm sorry sir," Blocker said, tightening his grip. "I'm not allowed to let you out of my custody at this point."

"I don't understand," the quaking man said, and Blocker led him away without a struggle.

When they got downstairs, the rental car was parked on the street in front of baggage claim, the man's wife and daughter waiting for him at the curb. Loreen and Mary Ann were parked a discreet distance behind in Olivia's black Lincoln.

Blocker hustled everyone into the car before a lot of questions could be asked, making Migliazzo drive while he explained to the horrified women about the unfortunate fire. Esther Migliazzo wasn't as easily convinced as her husband.

"Are you arresting us?" the woman asked.

"No, ma'am," Blocker returned as her husband got out of the airport proper and turned the Cougar onto Highway 101 north. "This is just routine."

"It's not my routine," the woman said. "You can't make us go anywhere without a warrant for our arrest. I know my rights. I'm not letting you get me in any police station without a lawyer so you can ask me anything you want."

"I assure you, Mrs.—"

"No," the woman objected. "You either arrest us or get out of our car."

Blocker had to take out the gun then. He would have preferred to wait, but it wasn't working out. He would have shot the woman on the spot but didn't want to mess up the rental car.

She began to scream and tried to roll the window down. Blocker was forced to lean over the seat and pistol-whip her with the automatic until she was unconscious, which started the daughter crying. Migliazzo, by this time, had the car all over the street.

They had to pull over.

Blocker opened his window and motioned for the Lincoln to pull ahead and find a parking place. They were moving along the inner harbor area, and there were sections of vacant beach on the right. He would have to go off there and move quickly.

Mary Ann pulled off at the first available exit ramp, then left the access road to go overland. Blocker hated the way this was coming off, but it was all movement now, fate declaring their moves.

He followed, his gun to the man's temple.

They passed several beachfront houses, then hit a hundred-yard stretch of open sand. He pulled up next to the Lincoln; Mary Ann and Loreen were already out of the car.

"Help me with the woman," Blocker said, trying to heft the unconscious bulk out of the back seat. "Come on."

The daughter kept crying, her excess weight jiggling with the movements. Blocker and John Migliazzo were struggling with the inert form of his wife, the man praying out loud as they gracelessly stuffed the woman into the Lincoln's back seat.

"I'm supposed to be her?" Mary Ann asked, looking with distaste at the daughter. "She's ugly!"

While Loreen prepared a large handful of C-4 to detonate by remote control, Blocker was hurrying father and daughter into the Lincoln.

The man sat behind the wheel, the daughter climbing in next to him, tears streaming down her ample cheeks.

"Now please stop crying," Blocker said to the girl. "We're not going to hurt you. What's your name, sweetheart?"

"Z-Zenna," the woman said, sobbing loudly.

"Let me have your identification, Zenna," Blocker said, taking her purse from her as she started to open it. "And you, sir. May I have your identification?"

The man reached into his back pocket and withdrew his wallet. "You're not really with the police, are you?" he asked.

Blocker just stared at him in amazement. "I want your wedding ring, too," he said. "Mary Ann. You get the ring from Mrs. Migliazzo."

"I don't want to be called Zenna," Mary Ann said, pouting as she pulled the ring off the comatose woman's pudgy finger.

"I'm ready," Loreen said, holding up the package of explosives.

Blocker turned angrily toward her. "That's right, advertise it," he said.

Just then, the engine started on the Lincoln, the man putting it into gear.

"What the—"

The Lincoln started across the sand.

"You left the keys in!" Blocker yelled, then aimed carefully through the back window of the departing vehicle and took a quick, soundless shot that burst through the glass.

The car rolled another twenty feet, then stopped. They charged the auto and found Zenna crying and hugging her father's body, which still sat in the driver's seat, the top of the head gone.

"You're ugly and you've got an ugly name," Mary Ann said, and put two shots into the woman's face.

"Come on, let's go," Blocker shouted, taking the C-4 from Loreen and tossing it into the back seat.

They ran back to the rental car and climbed in, Blocker driving. He geared out and tore through the sand, kicking large streamers behind the spinning back wheels. As soon as they made the access road, he nodded to Loreen.

The woman took the detonator out of her purse and turned the juice on. When the red "go" light started to blink, she flicked the switch, and the plastique exploded, taking the gas tank with it.

A huge orange fireball spread out fifty feet from the car, charring whatever evidence there was. It was easy for them to get back on 101, since a series of wrecks caused by people craning their necks to see the explosion effectively blocked the highway.

Blocker nosed the Cougar toward San Francisco in general, and Nob Hill specifically. It felt good, clean, to have another identity, other credit cards, other IDs. He'd never much liked Italians, but what the hell. Life was too short to spend it being prejudiced.

One thing Mary Ann was right about, though: Zenna was a terrible name.

14

Bolan stepped off the elevator and into the hotel lobby. Two hours of sleep had done him a world of good. He was more alert and calmer than he'd been since this business had started. The fact that wheels were rolling to get him tossed out of the project didn't bother him in the least. If it, indeed, happened, he'd work it his own way. Ultimately Joan Meredith had been absolutely right—he couldn't control the world, only himself. And ultimately every human being has to answer for his own actions and no one else's.

And perhaps Trevans was right. Perhaps Freon was on the run right now. If that were the case, he'd probably be caught before he could get out of the country. Despite everything else, some of the news had been encouraging. Though the denials continued to pour from the colonel's lips, the President wasn't buying any more and had said he'd hold the Libyan leader personally responsible for any more terrorist problems within U.S. borders. The President had put it quite succinctly when he'd said, "God will judge us on what we do here today." Amen.

Bolan looked for his people. Three men were stationed around the vast lobby, all casually keeping an eye on loiterers. They read, or chatted from the various conversation pits. They were supposed to look like customers, not cops, and were doing an exceptionally good job.

The afternoon's run of early customers were beginning to arrive; the check-in through the metal detectors and X-ray machines seemed to be going without a hitch. The only alarm so far had been from a man they'd caught trying to come in with a concealed .38. It turned out the man was wanted and had a long police record. He was turned over to the local authorities quietly, with most of the guests never knowing anything had happened.

Bolan moved around and made silent contact with each of the agents, then walked to the desk to talk to Higgins.

"Everything okay?" he asked the man.

"Yes," Higgins cooed. "Will you still be needing the Top of the Mark for the press dinner?"

"Press dinner?" the big man asked.

"It was scheduled by Mr. Pierce this morning."

"I'll check," Bolan said, angry. They had blown the cover while he was asleep. If they had already told the press, there was nothing he could do about it except hope for the best. He had halfway expected something like this.

"Well, please let us know quickly. We have to prepare."

"Yes, we will."

Bolan felt the strangest tingle, like a dark cloud passing before the sun. He looked around. An older man, his wife and punkish daughter were checking in beside him; people accompanying a porter brought a huge stack of luggage through the front doors. Nothing seemed out of the ordinary. "Have there been any cancellations? Anyone try to check in without a reservation?"

"Everything's normal, Mr. Belasko," Higgins said, and moved to take the credit card from the man beside Bolan. "Good afternoon, Mr. Migliazzo. I hope you had a pleasant flight?"

"Can't complain," Blocker said in his old man's voice, piercing Bolan with a stare as he walked away from the desk. He wanted to rip the Glock out of its belt holster and do the son of a bitch right on the spot, but he waited, biding his time. He'd get them all at once, right after that...what did they call it?—press dinner.

"Daddy?" Mary Ann said from beside him, and she, too, was watching the big man. Her eyes were wide, her body vibrating.

"That's him. Soon, honey," Blocker said, patting her hand. "Very soon."

They finished the check-in procedure and had a porter take their bags up to the elevator, where they went through an X-ray machine. The C-4 had been molded to fit the inner contours of the suitcases and the smoke bombs had been relabeled and topped to appear to be cans of hair spray.

"Excuse me, sir," the X-ray operator said. "What is the purpose of those canisters in your daughter's suitcase?"

"Look at her hair, son," Blocker said resignedly. "Disgusting. But she needs lots of hair spray to keep that damned crap in place."

"My hair isn't crap, Daddy," Mary Ann said petulantly. "I won't have you put me down in front of people this way!"

They were beginning to get quite loud, the X-ray operator looking around.

"Now you listen to me, young lady—"

"You may go on, sir," the operator said. "Everything's fine here."

Blocker looked apologetic. "Oh...of course. Sorry for the disturbance."

They took the elevator up to the fifth floor, the porter standing silently at attention next to his wheeled baggage horse. When they reached five, they got out, and the porter led them to room 511. Blocker tipped him with four dollars of Juicy's money.

Once inside, Mary Ann threw herself on one of the Victorian beds, pulling her weapon out from under her floppy shirt. "I thought I'd *die* going through the metal detector with this thing strapped on," she said.

Blocker smiled sadly. "I could always depend on Juicy. I think I might miss his fat ass."

Loreen had gone to the window and was staring out at the breathtaking view. "How the hell are we supposed to get out of here after we're done?" she asked.

"I figure to time it," Blocker said. "I heard them say at the desk that the press dinner was from five to seven. Check the man's itinerary and see if he has a rally in Chinatown at 7:30 tonight. If we set up right, we can hit him in the lobby leaving the dinner. Mary Ann can wait out front with the car running, as if we were just getting ready to leave for a show or something."

"Fair enough," the woman said, searching through her handbag for the written itinerary they had gleaned from the newspapers.

Blocker pulled a suitcase up on the vacant bed and zipped it open, pulling out a long strand of plastique. "Start tearing down that damned radio," he told Mary Ann.

The girl pulled the ghetto blaster onto the bed and unscrewed the back with a thumbnail. The electronic detonators, plus the transmitter, were jammed in with the relays and circuit boards.

Blocker peeled back the C-4 covering just a bit. "This much," he said, "baseball size. Each with its own transmitter. We're going to spread these around the lobby when we've got the chance."

"I think I spotted heat in the lobby," Loreen said.

Blocker nodded thoughtfully. "Yeah. We're going to have to figure a way around that. Belasko's got it locked up pretty tight. I can't figure out why he scheduled an event here, though. He's timed out the hit for us."

"Chinatown," Loreen said absently, then looked at him in confusion. "Did I hear you telling the colonel's people on the phone that you were going to meet them tonight?"

Blocker moved to the mirror, looking at his disguise. He looked older, but still virile. It would do. "That's what I told them. I figure by this time their orders are to kill us. So I'll keep them in reserve in case we need to set up a diversion later."

"You've set them up," she said, unable to keep the admiration out of her voice.

"No," Blocker returned. "They'll be setting themselves up."

Mary Ann was busy pulling off sections of C-4 and implanting detonators. "We get to kill him tonight, don't we?" she asked. "I almost went after him in the lobby."

"Tonight," Blocker said, "we avenge your brother's death."

"I want to do him close in," she said, her sweet face twisted grotesquely. "I want his blood on me."

Blocker smiled at her. "Whatever you say, sweetheart. Now, I've got to go out for a while."

"Out where?" Loreen asked.

He walked to the door. "Business," he said over his shoulder. "Stay here."

He moved out the door and strolled casually back to the elevators before she could protest. Getting out of this one was going to be a bitch. It was time to feather the nest a little bit. The way he was getting ready to be on the run, traveling light was the key, no excess baggage. He'd miss Mary Ann, but not Loreen. Besides, ten million spent a lot better undivided. Mary Ann had been his for a long time, but as she grew older, matured, she'd probably find a man; all women did. And then the mix would change. No, it was better this way.

He took the elevator down to the lobby and headed straight for the bar he had passed coming in. It was an elegant place, done up in brick, with filtered sunshine pouring through huge skylights. Quite pleasant. Quite civilized.

He walked in and stood in the opening for a few seconds, having to make an immediate decision. An older man sat alone at a corner table, drinking a tall lady's drink. He seemed to spend a second too long giving Blocker the once-over, and that sealed the decision.

Blocker walked unhesitatingly to the man's table. "I'm usually not this forward," he said, "but I'm new in town and don't know anybody." He smiled at the man and looked steadily into his eyes. "And I hate to drink alone."

The man stood and extended his hand. "Alistair Drew," he said. The men shook hands, the touch lingering until they had both sat down.

THE TOP OF THE MARK had been a tradition since World War II, when American soldiers embarking for the Pacific from San Francisco all wanted to have one drink at its dizzying heights to say farewell to their native land. Located above the top floor of the Mark Hopkins, the club afforded an intoxicating panorama of a fantasyland, complete with suspension bridges and a beautiful ocean view.

As Mack Bolan stood by its front door watching members of the nation's press corps file into the posh club, he was thinking of another war, a modern war, that America was trying hard to forget. She wouldn't be able to.

Carl Trevans was blustering around the club as if he were in charge, and Bolan had the feeling the man probably had some inside information. The big man had tried to play the bureaucratic game and come out a loser. Not surprising. Bureaucracies were run by the fainthearted, not the strong, their aim not progress but the maintenance of the status quo.

Joan Meredith, wearing a flower-printed sling for her broken arm, wandered in to stand beside him. "They really did it, didn't they?"

"Yeah, they did," Bolan replied. "And I don't think they have any idea of what they could be setting in motion."

"Denial is the first law of human action," she said. "If you ignore a problem, it will go away."

"It won't happen this time."

"You hear anything from Washington?"

"Not yet."

"Mr. Belasko!" an agent called from the doorway of the club office. "Phone for you. It's urgent."

"Guess I spoke too soon," Bolan answered, and moved toward the door.

"Belasko," Joan called, and he turned to her. "Good luck." She had her fingers crossed.

Bolan went into the office and took the phone. The ambience of the room was old-timey, like the rest of the building, its ornate brass fixtures and delicate wainscoting seemingly at odds with the computer and telephone systems on the old wooden desk.

He put the phone to his ear. "Belasko," he said.

"Striker, it's Brognola. I've got some bad news for you." Hal's voice was as taut as a bowstring. This entire incident had made him bone weary. "You're being pulled off this assignment. Everyone's complaining, from the candidate to the agents to Torrance's campaign committee. They feel you've exceeded your authority, that the events don't warrant the treatment you've given them."

"I've been following police reports," Bolan said. "They found a Lincoln with three bodies in it blown up on the beach. The bodies were burned to a crisp, but they salvaged the license plate. They're trying to connect the vehicle to a woman who was strangled sometime last night. I think Freon has established another identity."

"They'll need more proof than that," Hal said wearily.

"Hal, I *know* he's still out there."

"I'm sorry," Brognola responded. "The President wants me to thank you for all you've done so far in exposing this man to the government. But the consensus here is that Freon is on the run and that the precautions you've taken are too elaborate. With the threat ended, there's no reason why regular channels can't handle security."

"Hal—"

"Take a night off, you and Meredith. Enjoy San Francisco, then catch a flight back here tomorrow."

"Hal, listen to me, dammit!"

"There's nothing else to say, Striker," the man said, his voice strained. "I've been through the wringer on this, too. I'm sorry."

"Yeah," Bolan said, hanging up the phone. He turned around to see Trevans leaning against the doorframe.

"Told you I'd get you," the man said, grinning. "You can't stay in the game if you don't know the rules."

Bolan stared at him stonily. "What happens to all the security?"

"To begin with, we get rid of all the extra people you've got hanging around—the plainclothes cops out on the street and the Secret Service in the lobby. I'm putting them out in Chinatown where they can do me some good tonight."

"You're leaving the hotel unsecured?"

The man's face reddened in anger. "I never leave *anything* unsecured!" he shouted. "We'll have the regular contingent of personnel with the senator. Life is returning to normal, hotshot. All your bull is going out the window. I can do my job. Now get out of here. You're interfering with my security."

Bolan brushed past the man, holding in the urge to take his head off. He met Joan in the foyer, his expression telling her all she needed to know.

"Both of us?" she asked.

He nodded. "Hal said we should enjoy the city tonight and fly back tomorrow."

"Come on," she said, leading him out of the club to the elevator.

"Where are we going?" he asked.

"I've stashed a bottle of Scotch back in the suite. I think a good belt might help both of us right now."

The elevator opened, and the two of them stepped inside. "All things being equal," she said, pressing the down arrow, "you should feel relieved that you're out of this rathole."

"Yeah, I know," he said. "That's the part that bothers me the most. I can't shake the feeling that everything's coming down on top of us."

15

Loreen sat on the big overstuffed couch in the lobby and pretended to read a newspaper she'd found there. She glanced around the edges of the paper to see if anyone in the sparse lobby crowd was watching her. Then she casually reached into her purse and rolled out a ball of C-4, stuffing it down between the cushions of the sofa.

She glanced at her watch. It was nearly 7:00 p.m. Mary Ann had gone outside to bring the car around to the hotel entrance. The planting of the explosives had turned into the easiest part of the hit. For some reason, one of the American agents had come to the lobby and pulled his security. So, she and Mary Ann had simply wandered around the large room, looking at the paintings that hung on the walls and planting C-4 in sofas, chairs, free-standing ashtrays and assorted foliage.

Loreen had developed a sense of fatalism about this whole project. It had become too complex, too dependant upon Blocker's resources to suit her. He was up to something, but everything was moving too fast for her to put a finger on it. She had always fallen back on duty when things became too complicated, and she was doing that now, but she was beginning to think about her own mortality. If death were awaiting her, she'd meet it head-on, taking as many of the bastards with her as she could. That in mind, she left her last package of plastique in her handbag.

She stood, smoothed her skirt, moved to a house phone and dialed their room number.

The phone rang ten times before Blocker answered it.

"Everything's set," she said, and could see Mary Ann pulling up outside the doors at that moment.

"Good," he replied. "I just went upstairs and tried to get a drink. The Secret Service kicked me out, but I got a look in the room and everything's breaking up in there."

She felt her blood race, the familiar excitement beginning to take over. "Then get your ass down here," she whispered urgently. "We've got business to take care of."

BOLAN SAT WITH HIS SHOES and jacket off, feet propped up on a coffee table, and nursed his Scotch and water. He was trying to relax, to put this incident behind him, but it wasn't easy.

Joan sat on a sofa across from him, stockinged feet propped on the same table, her own glass held up against her temple so the ice could work on her headache.

"So, how come you've never signed my cast?" she asked, holding it up, her voice showing the effects of the alcohol. "Everyone between here and New Mexico who could claw a pen has marked the damned thing up, except you."

He shrugged. "Nothing to say, I guess."

"I get it," she said. "The strong, silent type."

"I want you to know," Bolan said, frowning, "that if this business hurts your career at Justice, I'm sorry."

She snorted and took a drink. "You don't get it, do you, you thickheaded idiot? I'd chew nails to be with you right now. I don't care if Justice flushes us both down the toilet. I've spent my life looking for a man like you, and when you come along, you're so wrapped up in duty you can't even see the hole you dug and pushed me into. Just my luck." She finished the drink and put the empty on the table.

A thought was just beginning to form in Bolan's mind when the phone on the coffee table rang. He leaned forward to answer it.

"Don't do it," she said. "We don't work here anymore, remember?"

He stopped, letting it ring again, then again. "I can't." He picked it up. "Belasko."

"This is Sergeant Meyers," an excited voice said, "SFPD. The captain asked me to call you."

"Yeah?"

"I think we found something."

Bolan was on his feet. "Go on."

"We definitely established that the car on the beach belonged to the woman who was killed last night," the man informed him. "Later this afternoon we got several calls from people in the neighborhood saying that a strange car had been parked out on that street all day. We investigated and found a Ford station wagon parked on the street a block from the dead woman's house. There was no registration, but we traced the engine block numbers back to a used-car dealership in Las Vegas...."

"Yes?"

"The car had been sold day before yesterday to a man by the name of Farley Masters."

"We've got him," Bolan said, dropping the receiver. He looked at Joan. "This is it!"

He ran to the door, Joan right behind, fumbling in her purse for her Uzi. She came out with the gun, the purse thrown aside.

They grabbed the elevator. "What's happening?" she asked as the doors closed on them.

"I've got hard evidence that Freon's here, in town," Bolan said, pushing the button for the lobby. "Those people dead on the beach were probably coming to this hotel."

"The computer system," she said.

"Right!"

The elevator stopped on the fourth, and several people started to get in, then backed off when they saw the gun.

They reached the lobby, the doors taking forever to open. Bolan ripped Big Thunder from the combat harness and ran out.

He saw it all in a glance.

Torrance, surrounded by Secret Service and a small cadre of reporters with TV cameras from the dinner upstairs, was moving through the lobby, ready to pass the registration desk. A man stood at the desk, seemingly chatting with the girl working behind it, while a woman sat on a sofa nearby, facing the desk. The entourage was getting ready to walk between the two— and into a cross fire.

"Freeze!" Bolan yelled, and the place went crazy.

Without hesitation, the man ripped a semiautomatic pistol out of his jacket and began firing into the crowd of newsmen, the woman picking it up seconds later.

Confusion reigned as the Executioner charged the scene, people screaming and running everywhere, the Secret Servicemen falling, Trevans pushing Torrance to the floor and covering him with his body.

The gunman jumped the registration desk, shooting the young woman behind it, using it for cover, as his accomplice leaped to the floor behind a pillar.

Jerry Pierce, uncomprehending, wandered around the scene, looking dumbly at the bodies on the floor, until the woman put two 9 mm parabellums in his chest and drove him into oblivion.

A newsman trying to film the scene on the run was gunned down by the hit man, his camera exploding in his face as he staggered, bleeding on the carpet, finally crashing into a potted palm and going down hard.

The Secret Servicemen rallied to Torrance, forming a cordon around him.

"Concentrate fire on the pillar!" Bolan shouted, making his way to the registration desk as Meredith maneuvered to get around behind the woman.

The concentrated fire kept the woman at bay, enabling Bolan to charge the long ornate desk, Blocker rising from behind, smiling, to take him one-on-one.

When Bolan was fifteen feet from the desk, he saw the car.

A teenage girl, her mouth open, screaming, had aimed a black Cougar at the front doors and jammed down the gas pedal. The car burst through the doors, glass and metal exploding loudly into the lobby. Bolan dived away from the desk to avoid the onrushing vehicle as it bore down on the agents protecting Torrance. The men jumped away and focused the field of fire on the car.

It happened in seconds. Bolan came out of a diving roll to pump AutoMag death at the careering vehicle. Loreen broke from the protection of the pillar to charge to the rear of the building.

Mary Ann was hit and jerked the wheel hard right, crashing through the desk and into the beehive behind, a tire on the driver's side jumping from the rim to bounce crazily through the lobby.

Bolan pivoted to the woman, but couldn't get a clear shot through the stand of pillars and shrubs. He saw Joan behind another pillar on a direct line, trying desperately to reload with her broken arm.

The girl, still screaming, tumbled from the wreck. She was covered with blood, her eyes like a crazed, wounded animal's. She brought her gun up and began to fire indiscriminately.

She was hit and hit again, then went down hard, limbs twitching crazily as she felt for her gun and began to return fire.

Bolan turned to the woman. Joan had thrown the Uzi to the floor and come around the pillar, swinging her cast. She caught the surprised woman head high, a loud crack audible even through the noise and screaming, Joan yelling out in pain as the woman went down heavily.

Mary Ann was up again, staggering, limbs flailing wildly as she fired, hitting an agent, fired, hitting an already wounded newsman.

Bolan opened up, catching her in the gut, throwing her back against the remnants of the registration desk as agents converged to hold her down.

Where was Freon?

Bolan ran to the desk and leaped over. Freon was gone. He turned to the girl. She was hard to control even with four men holding her down. She screamed and thrashed, her face set in a mask of total madness as obscenities spewed from her bloody lips.

She was over the edge.

"Smoke!" Trevans yelled from his position on the floor. Bolan turned in time to witness the destruction of the Mark Hopkins lobby.

Explosions rocked the room from a dozen different places. Like a string of firecrackers, the flashes followed one another in rapid succession, furniture and bodies blown across the room, windows crashing out. Tufts of white down floated in the air like man-made snow, and large chunks of the ceiling rained on all of them, forcing them to the floor.

And suddenly it was quiet—deathly still.

Then small sounds came up from the rubble, moans, the cries of the wounded.

Bolan stood, a large piece of plaster falling off his back and onto the floor. The room was a fog of smoke, with bits of down and foam still littering the air.

Men were beginning to rise, most covered with a fine coating of plaster dust. Many more lay on the floor, some never to rise again. The lobby of the Mark Hopkins had been transformed into an unrecognizable killzone, a nightmare vision, a fever dream of frightening proportions.

Bolan's thoughts turned immediately to his partner. "Joan!" he shouted, cupping his hands to his mouth. "Joan!"

He climbed out of the debris of the registration desk, maneuvering over a mammoth chandelier as he took out a handkerchief to cover his mouth and squinted his eyes against the sting of acrid smoke.

He stepped over bodies, nearly tripping over the corpse of Jerry Pierce, his face still locked in a gesture of surprise.

He moved farther, past an overturned sofa that had become entwined with a coffee table. A newspaper lay open on the floor, its pages turned to the comics.

And then he saw a figure staggering out of the gloom, Big Thunder coming up just in case. It was Joan.

She moved carefully toward him, her injured arm limp at her side, fingers twitching. As she got closer, he could see that she was covered with blood.

"Joan!"

He ran to her, taking her by the shoulders. "Where are you hurt?"

Her eyes were clouded, as though her thoughts were far away. Then, with an effort, she brought herself to the present. "The w-woman," Joan stammered, "she b-blew up."

She looked down at herself, shaking her head. "Her blood...her blood," she said, then collapsed into Bolan's arms.

16

Bolan slammed the door of the ambulance and watched as it took Joan down California Street toward San Francisco Memorial, the next ambulance in the line pulling up to take its place. There was a doctor staying at the hotel who had come down after the explosions to do what he could for the wounded. He'd performed an organized triage of the wounded, first sending out the most severely injured. It had heartened Bolan to know that Joan was the last live patient out of the devastation. In addition to her rebroken arm, the doctor had diagnosed a slight concussion, which Joan had received when she'd been knocked to the floor when the female terrorist had blown herself up.

The big man walked back through the huge hole that had once been the hotel's front entrance, passing a stretcher with a covered body going out. The final toll had been massive—nine dead, eleven wounded, not counting the two dead terrorists. Three of those wounded weren't expected to make it.

The smoke had cleared, and workmen were already moving through the ranks of police investigators and reporters to clear the rubble. The hotel management had done a quick check to make sure there had been no structural damage to the building itself, then decided to stay open for business, setting up a makeshift registration desk at the far side of the lobby, which was still intact.

Police were gathered near the wreckage of the car, searching the area for evidence. The police chief, Dodd, moved to Bolan. The two men shared a look of common sadness. Nothing more about the tragedy needed to be said.

Dodd held up an evidence bag that contained a semiautomatic. "Glock-17," he said. "Completely plastic."

"That's how they got through the detectors," Bolan answered. "The terrorist weapon of the future. Does the young girl have any identification?"

"Yeah. She has a wallet identifying her as Zenna Migliazzo. We've already checked that room. It was empty, clean as a whistle."

"You'll probably be able to match the name up with those dead people on the beach," Bolan remarked. "I think our boy broke into the hotel computer net when he killed those people on Beach Street the other night. He probably got the reservation name, then met the Migliazzos at the airport on some pretense."

"How does that tie with the dead woman on Lombard Street?"

Bolan noticed Jake Torrance talking with a group of reporters about fifteen feet away. "Once we exposed Freon's cover, he had to go underground. He probably picked her, killed her, then used her resources. Have you identified all the bodies?"

The man nodded. "They've all be accounted for."

"That means Freon's still out there."

"I'm afraid so." Dodd looked around, shaking his head. "We've talked to everyone who *could* talk. No one saw him get away. Your man Trevans pulled our stakeouts just before the incident, so we had no one on the streets watching for him. Have you got any ideas?"

Bolan looked at the man and saw the desperation that he wished had been there days ago. "It's out of control," the big man said. "He's a man who takes his job very seriously. Whether he'll try again or not is purely speculative. He may not have any more time to plan. He might be hurt. Remember, he still thinks he can get away with this, so he's going to work to protect himself, too."

"Do *you* think he'll try again?"

Bolan felt his jaw muscles tighten involuntarily. "Yes," he said. "At this point, I just want to get Torrance as far away from this place as possible. Freon wants Torrance—Torrance...and possibly me."

A look of exasperation crossed the man's face. "Then you'd better have a talk with your boy," he said. "From what I've heard, he plans to go on with his schedule."

"He can't."

"It's a free country, Belasko. I don't like it any more than you do, but there's no choice."

"Take him into protective custody."

The chief rolled his eyes. "A presidential candidate? You've got to be kidding."

"I'll talk to him."

"Do you have any suggestions for us at this point?"

Bolan shrugged. "He's probably on the streets, but do a room-to-room here just in case. Put five or six men in the lobby, and one in the Migliazzo room.

Freon still has his key. Don't let anyone in or out without searching them. Torrance will be the magnet. Concentrate everything on him.''

The man nodded. "I misjudged you," he said. "I'm sorry."

"I'm just sorry it had to end this way."

Bolan left the man and walked over to where Torrance was addressing a cadre of reporters. Politics was a world unto itself, its ebb and flow seemingly built on principles having nothing to do with human dignity or responsibility. Bolan was beginning to hate it, and what he heard from Torrance made him hate it even more. The man had gotten a slight cut on the head, and a thin trickle of blood ran down his temple. He had refused to wipe it off. Bolan wondered if any of the impassioned words he was hearing came from the man's heart.

"My campaign manager, Jerry Pierce, died in my arms," Torrance said as the cameras rolled, tears welling in his eyes. "And I knew, as I watched him gasping out his last breath, that I couldn't let his death be in vain. These animals are out to get me because I represent justice and vigilance, because the ideals I stand for will smash their kind like glass under our heels.

"I do not fear them because I am the arm of righteousness. Should I not survive, my message will. I will go on with my life, with my schedule, because it's important that we not bend to terrorism. We must stand up to it with a firm commitment in our minds and hearts. I am just one of you, but I will stand up to them regardless of the personal consequences to me...."

The man went on, but Bolan turned away. He'd heard enough. So Jake Torrance was ready to take a stand. What about the innocent lives he was putting in jeopardy because of that stand? Bolan's gut churned. He felt that Torrance was using this tragedy as a springboard to get himself a few more votes. Jerry Pierce, sure. Torrance hadn't been within twenty feet of Pierce when the man had died.

Well, it wasn't his problem anymore, at least not the Jake Torrance end of it. He'd be around, one way or the other, until Freon was caught; but this time he would be in the shadows. Bolan wouldn't quit on this. He couldn't.

He walked to the bank of elevators. Carl Trevans sat on the floor there, knees drawn up, face in his hands. He looked up with vacant eyes at Bolan's approach.

"Get up, Carl," the Executioner said.

The man stood slowly, his eyes searching Bolan's face. "You tried to tell me," he said, "to warn me. I was so...self-righteous and overbearing, so angry at you, that I did all the wrong things. I'm responsible—"

"The people who pulled the trigger are the ones responsible," Bolan said. "When the shooting started, you did the right thing. It took guts to use yourself as a shield that way. But don't blame yourself for what happened. Torrance and Pierce had a hand in your manipulation, too."

"Did you hear he intends to go on with his schedule?"

Bolan nodded. "How are you fixed for protection?"

The man took a breath and ran a hand through his disheveled hair, trying to get himself together through routine, through business. "We lost seven—four dead, three wounded. I've called down to the Chinatown people and have pulled some of them back here to act as bodyguards on the trip up. I also called Washington...."

Bolan narrowed his eyes. "And?"

"I took full responsibility and demanded that you be placed back in control of security until this is over. They agreed wholeheartedly." The man stuck his hand out. "If you'll have me, I'd still like to work with you."

Bolan shook the man's hand without hesitation. "I've seen the way you handle yourself, Carl. I can't think of anyone I'd rather have on my side."

BLOCKER LAY on Alistair Drew's bed at the Mark Hopkins, the telephone receiver cradled on his shoulder, his eyes glued to the television and the speech that Jake Torrance was giving from the hotel lobby. Blocker smiled broadly. He loved politics and its vacuum-tube logic; its allure made people do things that were completely contrary to good sense.

"Yeah, Emil," Blocker was saying. "It's gotten real hot for me here. I'm going to need some help getting out."

"Mr. Blocker," the man replied, his voice oozing sincerity, "we will be happy to help you. You have done us a great service. Just tell us where we may meet you."

"Someplace out in the open," Blocker said, "with large crowds. How about I take a trolley down California to Stockton in Chinatown. We'll meet near the trolley stop in thirty minutes.''

"That will be satisfactory, Mr. Blocker. We will take you to safety."

Blocker could hear Drew getting out of the shower. "Good. Thanks," he said. "I've got to run. Goodbye."

He hung up quickly, letting himself sink back into the bed. So far things were going as well as he could have expected under the circumstances. With Belasko and the rest of them occupied in Chinatown, he'd have the opportunity to plan something else here.

Drew came walking out of the bathroom wrapped in a towel and looked sternly at Blocker. "My dear man," he said, "I thought you were going to get dressed for dinner."

"I was thinking," Blocker said, "that perhaps room service might not be too bad tonight. I don't think the kitchen was damaged in the explosion. It would give us more time to...get to know each other."

The man's eyes narrowed. "You naughty, naughty boy," he said, then smiled. "Room service it is."

There was a knock on the door, then another.

"Who in the world...?" Drew began moving toward the door.

"I'll bet they're searching the rooms because of the trouble downstairs," Blocker whispered harshly. "Please don't tell anyone I'm here. I-I've got a wife, a family. I'd die if anyone knew...knew..."

The old man clucked his tongue. "Still in the closet, dear boy?" he asked, amused. "Well, don't worry, your secret's safe with me. Hide under the bed."

"Thanks, Alistair," Blocker said gratefully, rolling off the edge and sliding under the king-size bed.

Blocker watched Drew's bare feet pad up to the door. When the door was opened, he could see a policeman's shiny black shoes standing on the other side.

"Sorry to disturb you," the policeman said, "but we're conducting a search for a gunman involved in today's explosion. Have you see anything suspicious?"

"No," Drew replied. "As you can see, I'm staying here alone. No trouble."

"You've had no visitors?"

"Certainly not," the man said indignantly.

"Well, I guess that's it," the policeman said. "Sorry to trouble you. If you see anything unusual, call down to the front desk. We have a man stationed there."

Drew closed the door without further response and Blocker slid out from under the bed. He held the Glock in his left hand, out of view.

The older man moved to the bed and threw himself on it. "The hell with dinner," he said. "Let's see what's on the dessert menu."

"This is dessert," Blocker said, bringing up the weapon. He gave the man a second to appreciate what was going on, then blew his face away from point-blank range.

17

At nine miles per hour, San Francisco passed by Bolan's vantage point at a forty-five-degree angle. He stood in the back of the number 61 California Street cable car with Carl Trevans, traveling down hills so steep that he wondered how people could walk them.

This was the last leg of Torrance's swing through the city before tomorrow's primary, and it had been hurriedly planned in detail while Bolan was out of the picture. It called for Torrance, with local dignitaries, to take the cable car to Stockton Street in the heart of Chinatown and walk the length of the colorful block of shops and restaurants that was the central pivot of the largest Chinese population in the United States. Meeting the folks, as Torrance referred to it.

From there the candidate would be whisked away by armored limo to tour the Chinese Cultural Center and hold a brief rally. The part of the program that bothered Bolan the most was the walk down Stockton. Totally out in the open, the senator would be a target for any one of a thousand people. The SFPD had been very cooperative in this regard, stationing a large number of policemen along the route. Bolan's people would continually move through the crowds, keeping their eyes open.

American Nightmare

"You think he'll try anything else?" Trevans asked.

"I wish I knew," Bolan replied. "Organization will be his problem now. He's got no time to plan. A lot depends on his ability to improvise."

"Well, I'll be happy to get this part over with and get him back to the hotel," Trevans replied. "Now that we've beefed it up, it's the only place I'll feel safe."

The neighborhood began to change. The streets were filled with Chinese Americans now, and the houses, with their pagoda roofs and tiled fronts, had taken on more of an Old World flavor. Colored lights latticed from poles to buildings gave a festive air to the early evening. Banners in Chinese script were strung across the streets and hung from lightpoles. And as Bolan passed in the cable car, he could see gangs of Chinese youths watching everything with disdain. It was a world they were neither part of nor wished to be included in.

The gripsman rang the bell and called out, "Stockton!" as Torrance told some story to the press that made them laugh.

"God, I hate this," Trevans said.

Bolan remained silent, scanning the streets carefully as the car slowed to a crawl at the Stockton exit.

"Chinatown!" the gripsman called, pulling back hard on the big brake lever, the car squeaking loudly as it shuddered to a halt.

"Mike, that car," Trevans said, pointing.

"I see it," Bolan returned, feeling the knot in the pit of his stomach. A beat-up Cadillac was parked half a block up the street, men craning their necks to watch the cable car from the front seat. "This feels all wrong."

"Over there," Trevans said, pointing to a dark man on the corner who wore a long overcoat and kept looking around nervously.

Police walked up and down Stockton. Bolan could see them, but this section was relatively unguarded.

"Another one," Bolan said, pointing to a man pacing nervously across the street. The Executioner turned to the front of the car. "Ladies and gentlemen, I must ask your indulgence for just a minute. Please move quietly to the floor. You, too, Senator. There is a small security matter we have to take care of before we can exit."

Bolan and Trevans moved out of the car and in the direction of the man in the overcoat. He saw them coming and turned to walk away, his coat flashing open to reveal the barrel of a shotgun.

"Stop right there!" Bolan called, jerking Big Thunder from his combat harness.

The man started to put his hands up as the Executioner approached cautiously. Suddenly Trevans's hands pushed Bolan hard, knocking him aside.

"Watch out!"

The Executioner fell, rolling, and saw a man in a second-story window with a small automatic. His burst chewed up the sidewalk and chopped into Trevans chest high, the man flying backward to crash against a parked car.

Bolan took the man in the window first, a head shot that spun him around and pitched him through the opening. He fell hard on the sidewalk in front of his friend with the shotgun.

The street crowds, screaming, broke for cover as police and Secret Servicemen converged on the area. The man brought up the shotgun, but he was caught in a withering cross fire from ten different guns. The slugs punched him backward then forward before he slammed down atop the body of his friend.

The nervous man across the street was firing rounds, but through it Bolan heard the screech of rubber, and he swiveled to see the Cadillac reversing hard, the man in the passenger seat sitting on his window frame and firing an Ingram at full-auto over the top of the car.

As hot parabellums tore into the cable car, Bolan went low, using parked vehicles for cover. The man across the street was yelling in Arabic as police bullets tore him from chest to hip.

Bolan braced his arm on the hood of a Mercedes and squeezed off a controlled burst that tore through the rear windshield of the Cadillac and threw the gunman backward, his gun clattering to the pavement.

The driver threw the car into Drive and jammed down the gas, screeching back down the long, steep hill, his passenger, wounded, hanging halfway out the window.

The Executioner took a breath, leading his target slightly, and squeezed off four quick rounds. The vehicle veered crazily along the street. It bounced across the cable line, sideswiping cars on the driver's side, then swerved back the other way, hitting more cars. The passenger was jolted out of his perch and fell to the pavement.

Bolan heard two tires blow, and the Cadillac flipped, then rolled noisily down the hill to crash in a pillar of flame at the intersection at the bottom of the hill.

If there were any more players, they weren't showing themselves. The sounds of the street began to return, slowly, people speaking in whispers as Bolan holstered his AutoMag and walked slowly back to the Stockton intersection.

He walked to where Carl Trevans lay, his body propped halfway to a sitting position by the car he had slammed against. He was dead, killed by the bullets meant for the Executioner.

Kneeling beside the still-bleeding body, he shut the open eyes with his fingertips and lay Trevans flat on the sidewalk, covering him with his sports jacket.

"He was a good man," a voice said above him.

Bolan looked up to see Jake Torrance staring down at him, reporters crowded around. "What would you know about it?" Bolan asked, standing.

"Mike, I..."

Bolan turned from the man and walked away, moving to join the police who kept the curious crowd away from the dead terrorists. "Casualties?" he asked.

"Just these punks," a uniformed sergeant said, "and your friend."

Bolan nodded.

"I don't understand this," the cop said. "They set this up like they weren't expecting anybody to be here. The sons of bitches never had a chance."

Bolan thought of Freon. "Maybe they just planned it too hurriedly," he said, and wondered if his quarry could have been in the car lying at the bottom of the hill.

"I sure as hell hope so," the man replied.

Bolan walked away then, watching Torrance doggedly continue his trek down Stockton, leaving another trail of bodies behind him. And as he walked, the Executioner couldn't get out of his mind the picture of the man with the shotgun. When he had looked at Bolan, his face had registered a look of—what? Surprise.

BLOCKER WAITED until it was completely dark before trying for the suite. He had two things going for him at this point: one, the hotel had been built in 1927 and had real, not thermopane windows; and two, the late Alistair Drew had booked a room on the ninth floor, one floor below the suites.

The hotel facade was bright white, so Blocker dressed in white to blend in. The clothes he took from Drew's wardrobe were a little baggy, but would do in a pinch.

He had taken the draperies down, jerking the pulley rope out of the rod and making himself a makeshift grapple with the base of one of the Victorian lamp fixtures on the night table. When he was finished he had a serviceable tool that looked like a work of art.

When darkness descended, he opened the window and climbed out on the ledge. By now, his maneuvering had hopefully taken care of the colonel's opposition and, perhaps, Belasko as well, leaving himself a clear shot at Torrance.

The wind was cold and heavy, buffeting him as he made his way across the twelve-inch ledge to the end of the building. At each open window, he looked carefully into the room to make sure no one could see him from inside.

He didn't know exactly which suite would house the candidate, but it made sense to him that they would choose the one farthest from the elevator, with his security and aides in between.

He inched as quickly as he could along the ledge, anxious to get to cover before he was spotted from the ground. When he neared the end, he could look up at the balcony that surrounded the suites.

He tossed the grapple, which missed the concrete edge of the balcony rail. He tried again, then a third time without success. On the fourth try the grapple hooked the rail. Blocker braced his feet against the facade and pulled himself up to the balcony and over the edge.

He walked cautiously to the sliding glass door. The draperies were closed, but no light shone through the gap between them, so he assumed the absence of light meant the absence of humans. The door was locked, but he jimmied it easily enough with his penknife and entered the suite.

He moved into the darkened living room soundlessly, then hurried through to the bedroom, going through the personal effects there until he was satisfied this was, indeed, Torrance's suite.

Moving easily now, with familiarity, he went back to the living room and eased up to the front door. He turned the handle ever so carefully, then pulled the door open just a crack, enough to see a Secret Serviceman astride a chair next to the elevator. The man was reading a magazine. Good. With resident protection, they'd be less likely to search the suite.

Then he began to look for a hiding place—of which there were many in a suite that large, though none would stand more than a cursory examination. Finally he settled for the cabinet beneath the wet bar. Because of the plumbing, there was no middle shelf in the cabinet and with a little work, he found he could squeeze himself into the space and get the door closed. At this point, it was simply a matter of waiting until he was alone with his victim. He'd do the man, then leave the same way he'd come. He could then go back to Drew's room, hide out all day, then quietly check out when the commotion had died down.

Nothing to it.

18

Bolan accompanied Torrance and the rest of the entourage as the politician made his final campaign stop. The soldier's mind was on Trevans, on Joan, and on the look on the face of the man with the shotgun. Something was wrong with the hit in Chinatown, but he couldn't get a handle on what it was.

Torrance, for his part, was exuberant. He had all the publicity in the world, was promoting himself heavily as a middle-class hero, braving certain death for the voters of the United States of America. His rally at the cultural center was jammed, and with all the press in attendance, Bolan couldn't imagine how any of the other candidates were getting any coverage at all.

Freon was still on the loose, though even Bolan had to admit that the last, sloppy shot had been done in such haste that the man was out of luck at this point. With no more public appearances scheduled, and the hotel sealed like an Egyptian tomb, he didn't know if Freon would be able to get another crack at Torrance before he was caught.

He called Joan while the senator was making his speech to find that she'd have to undergo an operation to repair the damage done to her arm when she'd struck the terrorist at the hotel, but that everything was expected to go well. She'd stay one day in the hospital after the morning operation for observation, but there was no reason why she couldn't get out of there the following morning to fly back to Washington with Bolan.

The big man wanted to put as much distance between himself and the candidate as he could. He'd developed an unreasonable dislike for Torrance, and the fact that the man now seemed the odds-on favorite to win the election unsettled him more than it should have.

After the speechmaking, Bolan rode back in the limo with Torrance, the man ebullient, seemingly more so with each death notched on his campaign gun stock. When they arrived back at the hotel, they got the word that two of the three men critically wounded from the hotel gunfight had died.

It did nothing to dampen the man's mood.

Most of the rubble of the hotel lobby had been cleaned up considerably. The wrecked car had been taken away, the blood had been removed from the carpet and workmen were busy rebuilding the registration counter and the front doors. Hotel life would return to normal, whatever that was.

Torrance and six bodyguards, including Bolan, rode the elevator up to ten. The man by the sliding doors looked up sleepily and smiled at them.

"Anything?" Bolan asked.

The man shook his head. "Sorry about Carl," he said.

"He was a good man," Torrance commented loudly.

Bolan wanted to hit him.

"You men have done a great job," Torrance said as he led them down the hall to the suite. "As soon as I get into the White House, you're all going to get cushy jobs. Honest to God, I'd have been killed by those bastards ten times over if it weren't for you men. Especially you, Mike. You've really broken your butt."

"I didn't do it for you."

The man's lips tightened. "I understand how you feel. It's been rough for all of us."

One of the men unlocked the door, two of them going in first to check out the place. The rest of the group followed after an all-clear signal. When the door was closed, Torrance held his arms out wide.

"We made it!" he yelled.

There was halfhearted applause; everyone else was finding it difficult to lift their spirits. Torrance went to the bar and pulled a bottle of champagne out of a small refrigerator.

"I've been saving this for my victory party," he told them, "but what the hell. Now's the time!"

He pulled a stack of paper cups off a bar shelf and poured champagne into each as he gave them out. When he came to Bolan, the big man refused to take a cup.

"I won't drink with you, Jake," he said, not caring who was standing there. "I despise everything you stand for."

"Suit yourself," Torrance said, jaw set hard. "But wait until you hear the uproar I cause over the way you handled my security. Jerry Pierce would probably still be alive today if you'd done your job."

"Your words mean nothing to me."

The man pointed a finger at him. "In Washington, words mean everything. You've just become expendable, Mike."

BLOCKER LAY BENEATH THE SINK and listened to Torrance and Bolan. His first inclination was to jump out and kill both of them, but he knew there'd be no quick exit from his cramped quarters and that his position was by far the inferior one.

Well, no matter. The security man was a secondary target. He'd have to worry about him at a later date. Right now, he had a job to do, and business always came before pleasure.

He lay, listening, until he heard the sounds of the Secret Servicemen preparing to leave. The men drifted out, to their adjoining suites, leaving only the sounds of Torrance preparing for bed.

He inched the cabinet door open, moving it carefully so that it wouldn't creak. As he slowly unwound himself out of the small space, he could hear Torrance running a shower in the bathroom.

The lights were out in the living area, the only light in the room spilling from the bedroom. Blocker stood slowly, taking several minutes to relax his tensed muscles and massage the blood back into his legs.

His thoughts drifted briefly to Vietnam. It was there that he discovered the power, the realization that the man who could kill without remorse or thought could control all human beings, all human institutions. All that went into civilization was built around the concept of human life and its sanctification. Whoever could disdain that life could control all he touched. He wasn't the only one putting that concept into practice. In fact, he was small potatoes in the scheme of things. Every corporation that operated on the "profit motive" did it on a large scale by using up its workers, building inferior products, polluting the atmosphere. Every ruler of every nation who could throw his citizens into war for profit or ideology did it. Every clergyman who preached that his religion was superior to every other religion did it. The only difference was that Blocker did it consciously. He didn't lie to himself.

He heard Torrance turn off the shower and slide open the shower curtain. He primed his weapon.

MACK BOLAN CROUCHED behind the sofa in Torrance's suite and watched the man uncoil, like a snake, from behind the bar. He had begun to plan this moment as soon as he'd realized their assailants on Stockton Street hadn't been expecting *them*. It was all a ruse, set up by Freon to throw him off the scent.

Bolan was a live nerve, combat senses alert, tingling, as he straightened slowly. Every movement became an exercise in self-control. This was no ordinary encounter with death; he was facing a master.

As Freon crept cautiously to the bedroom door, his outline silhouetted in the lighting from the bedroom, Bolan eased himself out from behind the couch. He was twenty feet away with a clear shot. He brought the AutoMag up into target acquisition, sighting on Freon.

He had only to release the safety. His thumb slid to the tiny flange . . . flicked it—

Freon dived to the floor, his senses alerted to the smallest sound. Bolan, surprised, fired and missed. At Freon's silenced muzzle-flash, Bolan dived, a line of hot fire searing his neck as he missed death by half an inch.

He crawled behind the sofa, the wall behind him exploding in a shower of plaster. Bolan stood up, another shot just missing, and brought the sofa with him, heaving it into the center of the room, charging behind it.

He veered away to the left, rolling into a coffee table, firing at shadows. He could hear Torrance's frightened screams coming from the bedroom.

"Game's over!" Freon shouted, and all at once the room was bathed in bright, harsh light.

Freon stood in the bedroom doorway, beside the light switch. He had a choke hold on Jake Torrance, his gun buried in the man's neck.

There was loud pounding on the doors to the outside, the other agents drawn by the gunfire. Freon smiled broadly.

"Tell them to go away," he said politely. "Please?"

"Move away from the door!" Bolan yelled. "He's got Torrance!"

The pounding stopped, the two men staring at each other from a distance of ten feet. The man seemed to be a glacier, in control even in the worst scenario.

"Now, Mr. Belasko," he said, "I want you to put your gun on the floor."

"And then both the senator and I are dead," Bolan replied, and brought up Big Thunder to draw a bead on the exposed portion of Freon's head. "I don't like the odds."

"I mean it, Belasko," he said. "I'll do him right now."

"Dammit, Mike!" Torrance yelled. "Do what he says, for God's sake!"

"No," Bolan said. "There's something you need to understand, Blocker. You want Torrance and me dead. I want you dead. I couldn't care less about Torrance. All he is to me is something in the way of you. Pull the trigger and I've got a clear shot."

"Drop the gun!"

Bolan forced a wintry smile. "Your move."

He did what Bolan thought he'd do, the only thing he could do and still stand a chance. He shoved Torrance hard toward Bolan, then came around with the Glock.

Bolan dived for the floor, both men firing simultaneously. Bolan's shot took the fleshy part of Freon's shoulder, throwing him up against the doorframe. Bolan doubled over in pain as Freon's shot deflected off the firing mechanism of his still-holstered Beretta. Shrapnel dug painfully into his rib cage.

The Executioner gave his mind to the pain for only an instant. His vision cleared enough for him to see that Freon's impact with the door had jarred his weapon loose. The man's eyes caught the gun's location just as Bolan was angling from his position on the floor for another shot. With deadly calculation, Freon turned and lunged for his nemesis instead.

He came down hard on Bolan, knee first, as the AutoMag discharged into the ceiling. Groin pain flared through Bolan's body, and Freon banged his gun hand against the broken coffee table, forcing Bolan to release it.

Bolan reached up through waves of pain to grab Freon's bleeding shoulder hard.

The hit man screamed like an animal and tried to roll away, the big man staying with him. There was no pretense of humanity left as the two men tore into each other, Bolan pounding again and again on the man's face. Freon's nose cracked, blood spurting from the left nostril. The man somehow managed to come up off the floor and grab Bolan's hair from behind, pulling, snapping the Executioner's neck back as he staggered around with his burden. Bolan twisted out of Freon's grasp and managed to get his hands around the man's throat, squeezing with all his strength.

Freon gagged, violently pitching himself to the side. They hit the curtained glass of the patio, breaking through with a loud crash to land heavily on the concrete outside.

Pain seared through Bolan's leg, and he rolled off the man, trying to stand, a jagged gash on his thigh oozing thick dark blood. Freon sprang from the ground, butted Bolan chest high, driving the big man back against the patio railing, next stop ten floors down, as the lights of San Francisco twinkled toylike in the background.

Freon hit him again, trying to finish it and take him over the side, but Bolan got his arms around the man and held tight, both of them nearly going over.

Bolan had Freon's arms pinned to his sides, rendering the man ineffectual. He pushed from the rail, moving them back inside through the broken glass, Freon desperately trying to use his own head as a weapon, banging it repeatedly on Bolan's jaw.

Blood filled Bolan's mouth, and he kicked into action. Still holding the man, he ran him up against the bar, hearing ribs cracking. He did it again and again until he felt the terrorist go limp in his arms.

He dropped him to the floor, then, exhausted, sank to his knees. Freon lay on the floor, gurgling blood, his glassy eyes dark with hatred.

Bolan leaned over the man. "Why?" he asked between ragged breaths. "Why Torrance...why the others?"

The man smiled slightly and coughed blood. "Vendetta," he said. "They...insulted the colonel's m-man...hood..." He tried to laugh, his face turning ashen. "For m-money, he..."

The shot was loud in Bolan's ear, Freon's head blown apart from an up-close blast from the AutoMag. The Executioner rolled away from the body and stared up at Jake Torrance, who held the weapon in a two-handed grip, his face set hard.

Torrance looked at Bolan and raised the gun again.

"So, what now, Jake?" the big man asked. "Do you kill me, too?"

Torrance warred with himself for a moment, then he dropped the gun on the floor. "Oh, hell," he said, slumping to the carpet. "I never meant for any of this to happen."

"Where does the money come in?" Bolan asked.

Torrance passed a trembling hand over his face. "We were invited to Libya to do a story," he said. "We were the first allowed in under the colonel's regime. He wined and dined us, then made us an offer." The man laughed, shaking his head. "Ten million dollars." He looked hard at Bolan. "Ten *mil-*

lion dollars. All we had to do was write a favorable story that would get him the airplanes he needed. He gave us the money in cash, U.S. currency. Who could turn down a deal like that? We filmed freely, then realized we couldn't do the story he'd asked us to do. So, the three of us made a deal: take the money, write the story we want and never look back. What was so bad about that?''

''Why didn't you tell us about it from the beginning?'' Bolan stood, picking up his gun. The Secret Servicemen had resumed pounding on the door.

''We had lives,'' Torrance offered, his voice pleading. ''We'd all used our cash to make good lives for ourselves. I didn't see any reason to jeopardize that. Where's the harm, Mike? Where's the harm?''

''You really don't see it, do you?'' Bolan asked, shaking his head. ''You're so caught up in all this that you don't see it at all. All the death, all the horrible death would never have happened after the first murders if you had only said something. People would have believed you. It would have made sense. We could have hidden you and the Blackman woman and stopped Freon in his tracks. Freon may have pulled the trigger, but you're the one who loaded the gun.''

''B-but I wanted to...get elected,'' the man stammered, burying his face in his hands. ''I just know I can do...so much good.''

Bolan walked toward the door. ''No, Jake,'' he said over his shoulder. ''You can't do anybody any good.''

''Are...are you going to tell what happened?''

Bolan put his hand on the knob, then stopped. ''I'll tell my contact in Justice,'' he said, ''because that's my job. But I don't think he'll say anything about it. I

don't know if the country could recover from the kind
of disgrace you've brought upon it.''

Then Mack Bolan opened the door, the outside
world flooding in.

19

Bolan hobbled on one crutch down the hall of San Francisco Memorial Hospital and pushed open the door to room 310. "Joan," he called, "are you dressed?"

"Yeah," came Joan's reply. "Too bad for you."

He entered the room, the woman smiling at him from her bed. Her arm was reset in a new cast.

"The President ordered another bombing raid on Tripoli last night."

"Thank God he stopped worrying about what the rest of the world would think." She clucked her tongue at him. "You look like a mummy."

"You get a little cut and they put you on crutches," he groused, hobbling up to the bed. "How do you feel?"

"I'm going to be fine," she said. "How about you?"

"Cuts, contusions, lacerations," he said casually. "The usual."

"Look," she said, pointing past him to the television. "Election results."

Bolan turned and looked at the TV. An announcer was standing in front of a big board filled with names. As he announced preliminary results, his face had a look of surprise. "It's difficult to believe, ladies and gentlemen, but out of a field of six primary contenders, our projected favorite, Senator Jake Torrance, is now picked to finish fourth. As near as we can analyze from here, it looks as if the voters have rejected the senator in large numbers, feeling that he has been using the terrible tragedies of the past week for personal gain. From where we're sitting, this is going to deal a serious, if not fatal, blow to the senator's hopes of becoming president...."

Bolan sat back in his bedside chair. "Maybe things aren't as bad in this country as I thought. The people sure had a good eye where Torrance is concerned."

"And the government had enough good sense to bring you back to the fold," she replied, reaching out her free hand to touch his arm. "I've said it before, you're a good man, Bolan, even if you won't sign my cast."

Bolan smiled slightly and thought about the small pleasures in life, the inconsequential things that made people happy.

"Bring your arm and that marker over here."

Mack Bolan's

by Dick Stivers

Action writhes in the reader's own streets
as Able Team's Carl "Ironman" Lyons,
Pol Blancanales and Gadgets Schwarz
make triple trouble in blazing war. Join
Dick Stivers's Able Team as it returns to
the United States to become the country's
finest tactical neutralization squad in an
era of urban terror and unbridled crime.

"Able Team will go anywhere, do anything,
in order to complete their mission. Plenty
of action! Recommended!"
—*West Coast Review of Books*

**GOLD
EAGLE**

Able Team titles are available
wherever paperbacks are sold.

AT-1

Mack Bolan's

PHOENIX FORCE

by Gar Wilson

The battle-hardened, five-man commando unit known as
Phoenix Force continues its onslaught against the hard
realities of global terrorism in an endless crusade for
freedom, justice and the rights of the individual. Schooled
in guerrilla warfare, equipped with the latest in lethal
weapons, Phoenix Force's adventures have made them a
legend in their own time. Phoenix Force is the free world's
foreign legion!

**"Gar Wilson is excellent! Raw action attacks
the reader on every page."**

—Don Pendleton